IRISH MIST

A Simon Rush / P. J. Porter Mystery 10-25-10

*Carla —
I hope you enjoy this story —
Knighton Meade*

BY

KNIGHTON MEADE

This is a work of fiction. All the characters, places, incidents and dialogue, except for incidental references to public figures and historical occurrences, are imaginary and not intended to refer to any living persons nor disparage anyone or any institution.

Published by Knighton Meade, dba Ballyduff Press.

All rights to this book owned by
Knighton Meade, dba Ballyduff Press
Copyright © 2010

1816 Drury Lane
Oklahoma City, Oklahoma 73116
Ph: (405) 843-1544 Ex. 222, or Ph: (405) 842-2217
Fax: (405) 848-8141
Email: ktmeade@meade-energy.com

ISBN# 978-0-615-37583-0

DEDICATION

To the Dead Writers Society of Oklahoma City and its peerless mentor, Carolyn D. Wall, who have enabled many seniors like myself to fulfill their dreams to write and embark on exciting new careers with stimulating new friends.

1

When my Aer Lingus flight leveled off at 20,000 feet, I stuffed the unused barf bag back in the seat pocket. I'm aviophobic – petrified of flying. I'd hoped that this condition would improve with time, but to my chagrin, it hasn't. At the age of twenty-seven, it was probably too late to change. But at cruising altitude, I stopped praying, sheepishly smiled at the bewildered man sitting next to me and relaxed enough to cell-phone police headquarters in Galway City.

I'd tried to telephone earlier when leaving St. Clerans but was informed I was too early – not only was Galway time an hour earlier, but the officer in charge, Sergeant Ross McConnell, "t'would not be on duty 'til mid-morn." What kind of policeman was this guy? Sounded more like a banker.

When I called from the plane, a man with an agreeable Irish lilt answered. "McConnell, Central Garda."

"Hello, this is P.J. Porter, a female police officer from the United States, calling in an unofficial capacity."

"What can I do for you, Porter?" Now he sounded unfriendly and inconvenienced. Would it hurt him to address me as *Miss* or *Officer*?

"I'm in a plane – flying to Shannon Airport from London. Friends of mine in the U.S. have asked me to check on a horse agent, Sean O'Malley, whose been charged with a crime. Do you know who he is?"

He hesitated then snarled, "I know O'Malley. What's your connection to him?"

"My friends, the Devereux family in Oklahoma City, had hired O'Malley to search for Irish show jumpers for their daughter, Kit. When they learned he might be in trouble, they retained me to check it out." No need to reveal that Mrs. Devereux had had a fling with O'Malley and was probably still pining.

"Do you have any I.D.?" he grumbled.

"Hold on." I riffled through my jacket and pulled out the few cards I was carrying. "Here's my Commission Card number – OCPD 2678-A39. Check it out."

"I will."

Officer McConnell must have covered the receiver and was speaking to another officer because I could hear muffled conversation. In few minutes he said, "Sorry, Porter. I can't offer much – O'Malley is dead!"

"*Dead*? When?"

"Two days ago. At the moment, we're calling it a suicide."

I shook my head in disbelief. The Devereuxs said

they'd just talked to him, less than a week ago. "What happened?" I asked.

At that moment, the plane hit an air pocket and dropped with a bang. "Oh my God!" I screamed, juggling the phone. The poor soul next to me, anticipating the worst, grabbed the sick-sack and presented it below my chin. I shot a glance across the aisle – the opposite passengers were wide-eyed, wondering what I would do next.

"What's going on?" McConnell shouted. He probably thought we were under a terrorist attack. To me, it felt like a mid-air collision.

I took a deep breath. "Sorry. I thought the plane hit something – just turbulence. I hate flying! Everything's fine."

"Good!" he barked. "If you arrive in one piece and want to talk to me, come by the office – I'll work you in. Galway City's two to three hours from Shannon. We're in the center of town – corner of Abbeygate and Market. The Shannon auto agent will give you directions."

I peered out the window to make sure the wing was still intact and nervously grinned at the gentleman next to me. He nodded with uncertainty, hesitated, then slowly folded and stored the unblemished bag.

"Sergeant, I'll rent a car and be there as soon as possible. Thank you," I said, but he'd already hung up.

2

I gazed out the window and searched for landmarks below. We were over Dublin, thirty minutes from Shannon, bouncing through intermittent clouds and showers. A dreary day which fit my mood.

Simon and I had shared a sentimental goodbye in the sculpture-filled garden of Grantham Castle, Leicester, England. We had just solved the murder of the Duke of Grantham's huntsman, as well as two attempts on the Duke's life.

Though Simon had remained in England to finalize business, he would be returning to the U.S. in two days to begin law school at Georgetown University in Washington, D.C. By sheer coincidence, we'd both selected the same law school because we wanted to taste the historic and political turmoil of our nation's capitol. I expected to join him there in three months as another late-blooming student.

To add to my fear of flying, I was distraught over being separated from that intelligent, irresistible man. We'd made a great investigative team which, in that parapet-crowned estate, had become complicated by an intense mutual attraction. Now I needed some distance from Simon and time to evaluate what I wanted from our relationship. We may have become too close to continue as business partners.

Without further incident, I arrived at Shannon, a minor league airport compared with Heathrow International, and picked up a rental car that Kit Devereux had reserved for me. One change would up her cost – I switched to an automatic transmission. The popular rental in Ireland was manual shift, but I didn't think I could cope with all that shifting while learning to navigate on the *wrong side* of the road. In England, Simon had done most of the driving.

The rental agent gave me a road map with directions to the Central Garda. I was told that it was only forty-five miles away, in the middle of Galway City, but that I should allow two hours. With that, I was off.

I soon understood why the short trip to Galway City required so much time. Outside the town of Ennis, I mistakenly picked up the *scenic route*. The roadway became narrow, barely wide enough for two cars to pass, and lined with intimidating, stacked-stone walls that I could almost reach out and touch.

Though the picturesque view of diminutive, lush farms was breathtaking, it seemed dangerous to take your eyes off the road. Rounding one turn, I realized that cars up ahead had abruptly stopped. I assumed there had been an accident which would further delay my mission. But this was not the problem. Traffic had halted to permit the crossing of a flock of bleating, wool-heavy sheep. I wondered what would happen if I were to blast my horn like a New York cabbie – probably a lynching, followed by an Irish wake. A black and white sheepdog hustled his charges along while keeping an eye on the cars.

As I waited for the road to clear, I considered my circumstances. Was being in Ireland worth my effort and Kit's money? Alone and stuck in traffic in a foreign country, on a quest to find a man who was now purported to be dead, I had my doubts. Contrary to the farewell pledge I'd made to suspend our relationship, I wished Simon were here to keep me company.

Simon and I had first met in Oklahoma City where I, as a somewhat inexperienced police officer, had solved, with his help, the death of his socialite girlfriend and also the brutal murder a barn worker. Maybe credit should be the other way round.

If I had a misgiving about twenty-nine-year-old Simon Rush, it was that he was built like a wide receiver, probably six foot two and two hundred pounds, with unruly blond hair that cried out for female attention. Till now, I'd steered clear of such tantalizing men because they weren't good, long-term bets – other women were always offering them bed and breakfast that most men couldn't resist. But from our first conversation in a stall at Trails End Stables, when I was interrogating him as a murder suspect and he was grooming his dead girlfriend's horse, there was an undeniable magnetism, enhanced by those wonderful barn odors that only horse-lovers, like us, truly savor.

And this affinity had survived the recent onslaught of a castle full of English aristocracy to this moment, barricaded by a flock of sheep in rural Ireland. Deep down, I don't believe either of us wanted to throw away the energy we'd discovered, just suspend it and see if it survives the test of another investigation.

Now, what was with this Sergeant Ross McConnell in Galway City? He sounded old and grouchy – probably waiting for his pension to come through and didn't want to be bothered with a foreigner. I'd been hoping that the assignment I'd volunteered to undertake for the Devereuxs would be hassle-free. I knew better, of course.

I'd met Kit Devereux and her flamboyant, divorced mother, Barbara, while investigating my first two murders in Oklahoma City. Kit was a young Grand Prix show jumper with great promise, and her vicariously ambitious mother was her sponsor, always on the prowl for an extraordinary horse to assure her daughter's success. This had led Barbara to Ireland and an affair with her horse agent, Sean O'Malley.

Just then, the sheep cleared the road, cars began to move and I snapped back to reality. Consulting my map, I found my way to highway N18 and soon approached the outskirts of the city overlooking Galway Bay. Despite a gentle breeze off the ocean, a mist hovered over the water. Seagulls circled above two commercial fishing boats, diving to gorge themselves on morsels tossed overboard. Sailboats on the bay seemed almost becalmed. The scene had a soothing effect and convinced me I was really in Ireland.

Galway City was not large by U.S. standards – about 65,000 people. But it was difficult to drive through because the streets were narrow and winding and mostly one-way. I spotted an underground parking facility, near what I guessed was the middle of town, pulled in and set out on foot to find the station. All the buildings in the shopping district appeared charmingly similar – two-story, white stucco with geranium boxes and brightly painted doors. There was one unusual difference from any American town of comparable size – the proliferation of colorful advertisements that seemed to adorn every building and street corner. But they weren't offensive – just part of the city's distinctive appeal.

I considered stopping in a pub to find the ladies' and spruce up, but then I thought, why bother to impress an ill-tempered Irish sergeant?

* * * * * * *

It was 1:00 p.m. when I found the Central Garda – a whitewashed, concrete-block building with the main entrance at one end and barred windows at the other. The cramped reception area appeared unattended. But when I approached the counter, I realized that a slight, elderly woman was bent over a desk on the other side. She wore a blond wig and granny glasses. Peering over the rims, she asked in an appealing accent, "May I help ye, dear?"

"I'm hoping to meet with Sergeant Ross McConnell. I'm Officer P.J. Porter."

From beyond an opaque glass partition, a man gruffly ordered, "Margaret, have Porter meet me at Blarney's. Give me ten minutes!"

Margaret creaked to her feet. "Yes, sir." Then pointing toward the window, she said, "Blarney Spoken Here is a pub across the street. You could have a nice cup of tea and a bite, miss."

I wanted to shout something back at the discourteous man behind the barrier but held my tongue. We could settle our differences later. "Thank you, Margaret," I groaned and stomped out the door.

Blarney's was on the opposite corner. Just inside the entrance, to the left, were swinging doors, leading down a dim hallway to the barroom. A sign over the corridor warned "The Truth Stops Here."

The dining area was to the immediate right. Lace café curtains lined the windows, shielding the patrons from curious pedestrians. The walls were white plaster, not the usual dark paneling, and decorated with hand-painted caricatures of leprechauns, colorfully dressed and engaged in various activities — like warming themselves by a fire, mending shoes and counting gold coins. Along the window a half dozen tables were enlivened with bright green cloths, white napkins and fresh flowers. I felt certain this was where McConnell wanted me to cool my heels.

Only one other table was occupied. Three ladies, wearing hats and enjoying cake and tea, whispered as if sharing some delicious gossip. Watching them made me hungry. I'd almost forgotten about lunch. A waitress, with a green ribbon tying her ponytail, and wearing a four-leaf-clover apron, seated me and took my order for tea with lemon and assorted, bite-sized sandwiches. After twenty minutes of nibbling, stretching my back and sighing, there was no sign of McConnell. I concluded that this entire trip had been a mistake and decided to pay and leave. As I was beckoning for my bill, a tall policeman, not much older than me, with his blue and white cap tucked under his arm, strolled into the pub and spoke to the hostess. She pointed toward me. Oh, God – not another hunk, I thought. I should have made that pub stop and brushed my hair. His thick, wavy black hair and prominent cheek bones made me wonder if he could be part Cherokee like me. Not likely!

I rose to greet him. His pace slowed as he studied me.

"I'm P.J. Porter," I said coolly.

His stern expression became a flirtatious grin. "Sorry to have kept you waiting. I'm Sergeant Ross McConnell." He extended his hand, and I accepted it. As we shook, he surprised me by placing his other hand on mine in a too friendly gesture. I jerked mine back.

I had a feeling this guy was going to hit on me hard before this inquiry was over.

3

McConnell motioned toward the table. "We can talk here." He fumbled to hold my chair. "Your flight sounded rough."

"I'm nervous about flying, but I'm here."

"Sorry I'm late," he said. I was struck by the deep cleft in his jaw – reminded me of George Clooney. "We have three other officers on duty today, but two called in ill, probably foxhunting, and the third is with the coastal wardens, looking for Sean O'Malley's body."

Once he'd adjusted his chair and appeared comfortable, I said, "Sergeant McConnell, let's get right to it. O'Malley's why I'm here. Can you explain what happened to him?"

"Certainly, if you'll call me Ross."

Though I wasn't in the mood to be friendly with this guy, it would accomplish nothing to be rude. "And I'm P.J."

Nodding, he plopped his cap on the table and waived to the waitress. "Kate, a cup of black coffee, please, and more tea for the lady." He turned back to me. "Where would you like me to start?"

"First, tell me what garda means? That's a new one."

McConnell smiled, showing off his brilliant, but slightly crooked, teeth. "Ah, yes. Garda is a Gaelic word. It means police or policeman. The plural is gardai. Anything else?"

"Well, you could begin with the crime Sean O'Malley's been accused of."

"I assume you know that he was one of the most successful sport horse agents in Ireland. And it's no secret, he was also a renowned ladies' man. Anyway, O'Malley had clients all over the world, mostly from America and mostly women. In this case, buyers from your Dallas, Texas, by the name of Farrell had purchased two nationally acclaimed show jumpers from Galway breeder Jimmie Craigh. They were insured for a million euros each – a total of almost three million dollars. The sale had been arranged by O'Malley, and he was responsible for the shipping. When the horses arrived in Dallas, it became obvious from their ability and further vetting that they were bogus look-alikes. The real items had vanished. That triggered the investigation."

"Was there credible evidence against O'Malley."

McConnell shifted in his chair. "We were working on that. We interviewed a half dozen people – all implicated him. Shortly after we attempted to bring him in for a second questioning, we learned that he'd committed suicide at the Cliffs of Moher."

"Ross, are you telling me he leapt his death when the police had no hard evidence?"

"There's more. We'd also received a report that the equine passports, which were in O'Malley's custody, appeared to have been forged. The case was just coming together, and that might have been enough to set him off. Now, it's my turn to ask you something."

"All right."

His friendly expression turned suspicious. "Tell me about your relationship with O'Malley."

Was he implying I might be another of O'Malley's paramours? What nerve! "As I told you, I was in England, finishing up a case, when I received a call from a friend in Oklahoma City, Kit Devereux, asking me to check on O'Malley on my way back to the U.S. A few months before, Kit and her mother had retained O'Malley to locate some quality show jumpers. Kit's an aspiring amateur with her eye on the Olympics....or maybe that's her mother's ambition. Anyway, when they learned that their horse agent was in trouble, they hired me to look into it, so here I am."

"And your friends had no interest, financial or otherwise, in the two horses gone missing?"

"As far as I know, absolutely none."

"Are you aware that Lloyd's of London has offered 70,000 euros, $100,000, for information leading to the recovery of the missing horses?"

"No, I've not heard that. McConnell – excuse me,

Ross – believe me, I know little about this case. I had no idea O'Malley was dead. The Devereuxs just asked me to detour to Ireland and inquire about him. That's all."

He nodded and leaned back in his chair. "I believe you. Now, how can I help?"

I took a sip of tea. "Kit and her mother will want to know more. If I wouldn't be interfering with your work, I'd like to see the place where O'Malley jumped to his death?"

"You wouldn't be interfering. I'll be motoring down there tomorrow to meet with Chief Warden Paddy Nolan. You're welcome to tag along. It's a scenic drive along the coast, less than an hour away. Where are you staying?"

My frustration with Sergeant McConnell mellowed. Must be the disarming blue eyes and Irish brogue. "The Devereuxs made a reservation for me at a house outside of Galway City – St. Clerans. Do you know it?"

His jaw dropped. "P.J., St. Clerans is no ordinary house! It's the former manor estate of your famous movie director John Huston. It's very exclusive and has a fabulous restaurant – not frequented by local peace officers."

"Well, she can afford it and probably wanted to make sure I was comfortable."

"Ah, you'll be that – and then some. If you find my help satisfactory, you could invite me to dinner?"

"Sounds like a bribe."

"Call it a trade off."

"We'll see." My opinion of him had improved, but he wasn't out of the woods, yet.

4

St. Clerans lay thirty miles east of Galway City, off the highway to Dublin. At dusk, I was fortunate to spot the weathered, set-back sign indicating my turn. There was no gated entrance – just two miles of narrow, winding road through dense woods and over one-lane bridges. To try and find this place at night would have been near impossible! But McConnell was right – St. Clerans was no bed and breakfast.

This stately 18th century Georgian mansion was set in a clearing, overlooking forty-five acres of lush pasture with grazing horses. It had been acquired by John Huston, the American film giant and father of Anjelica Huston, in 1954. He was an avid foxhunter and discovered the house while out with his favorite pack, the Galway Blazers. It was love at first sight – just the place to raise his family and entertain his international circle of hunting and drinking pals.

In 1971 the mansion was purchased by Merv Griffin, another Hollywood American, to add to his worldwide stable of unique resort hotels. He converted the interior into distinctive reception rooms, twelve luxurious suites and a five-star restaurant.

Now a young man, nattily dressed in a Black Watch jacket, navy slacks and Kelly-green necktie, escorted me to the *Griffin Suite* – two queen-sized beds, a sumptuous bath and a large sitting area furnished with antiques and lined with bookcases, containing reading materials and memorabilia, including pictures of the Huston and Griffin families.

After ordering dinner in the room, I began unpacking my duffle. I was startled by a noise outside my curtained patio door. "Who is it?" I called.

No answer, only the rattling of the door, like a drunken guest, searching for his room.

I edged closer. "Who is it?" I repeated.

Still no answer. Should I call the front desk? I decided to take a peek, first. The patio was illuminated by a soft floodlight. I was startled to see that the demanding caller was one of the largest brown and white horses I'd ever seen – nearly eighteen hands. He looked at me with huge, sad eyes that seemed to say, *I'm lost. Would you keep me company?* Or, *I'm famished – could you spare a bit of hay?* He continued bumping his nose against the door, but I wasn't about to open it.

Backing away, I grabbed the phone. "This is Miss Porter in the Griffin Suite. There's a huge horse on my patio!"

"Oh, goodness! So sorry!" The clerk laughed.

I wasn't amused.

"Tis Clancy himself. Naughty boy jumped the bar ditch again. I'll send O'Leary around to collect him. Sometimes Clancy has the courage to leap across but not back. He's harmless – just looking for human companionship. We'll attend to him."

"Thank you. He did surprise me, but I understand – except the part about the bar ditch."

"When you look around in the morning, you'll see that it acts as a fence, without rails. Except in the case of Clancy, it works quite well. Sorry for the fright. Have a good night's rest."

"Thank you."

As I enjoyed my "light supper" of Pan Fried Fillets of Sea Bass with Braised Fennel and a Green Salad, I telephoned Kit to report on Sean O'Malley. Despite the expense, she asked that I spend a few more days at St. Clerans to gather what information I could about O'Malley's death. Her mother was going to be upset and would want more details. Also, Kit advised me that the Farrells from Dallas, the people who had been swindled, were offering a hundred thousand dollars to anyone who could recover their Irish jumpers. With the hundred thousand from Lloyds, there was an enormous amount of money at stake. Maybe I could work on that while investigating the death of O'Malley. But I would need to discuss this with Simon – he could deal with the Farrells in the U.S.

Simon was planning on leaving Grantham Castle tomorrow. I would call him right now. He ought to be in his room unless he was spending his last night with Emma Ferguson-Sloan, the refined divorcee he'd met in England.

5

"Hello, Simon, this is your partner checking in," I said when he answered my cell call. "Can you talk?" I was being sarcastic, but at the same time suspicious that he might be with Emma.

We'd met Emma Fergusson-Sloan on our first night in Grantham Castle at a dinner party thrown by the Duke of Grantham. She was from landed gentry and a remarkable look-alike to Simon's now-deceased girlfriend, Selina Norman. Simon and Emma had made an immediate connection. This was unfortunate because he and I were becoming more than business associates. But I was prepared for this sort of dalliance because Simon Rush was a macho guy that most women drooled over.

Emma owned and operated an historic, two-hundred-year-old estate. Despite this and her stunning rural beauty, her RAF pilot succumbed to the allure of foreign duty and abandoned her. A year later, they were divorced.

She had been courted by several worthy suitors whom

she'd rejected out of hand. When Simon appeared, that all changed. It took all my self-control to shut up and let their star-crossed attraction run its course.

"Hi! I was just thinking of you," he replied. "How are things going?" If Emma had been there, I doubt he would have been so light-hearted.

"Things are going well, but I have a lot to report. Where are you?"

"I'm at the castle – getting ready for bed. I spent the day with Emma and said goodbye – for the last time – I think. Details to follow."

I was tempted to ask questions but didn't. "Sounds good. Bad news here is that Sean O'Malley is dead – suicide, they're saying."

"Really!"

"Still haven't found the body. Kit wants me to stay a few days longer and check it out. O'Malley was supposed to have jumped off a seven hundred foot precipice called the Cliffs of Moher, which I find hard to believe. Anyway, I've arranged to travel down the coast tomorrow with Sergeant McConnell to see where it happened."

"Who's Sergeant McConnell? Sounds like he's very accommodating." He chuckled.

Why should he care – he had Emma.

"He's the officer in charge." I attempted to sound indifferent. "He was driving down anyway."

"By the way," I said, changing the subject, "between Lloyds of London and Tex Farrell of Dallas, there's a two hundred thousand dollar reward for recovering the stolen horses. I thought we might pursue that while I'm inquiring about O'Malley. Someone will have to talk to the Farrells in the U.S., and you'll soon be there. What do you think?"

"Sounds good, but first, I need to register at law school. I'll do that in a day or so, then see how much time I have. But – where would you like me to begin? The horses could be anywhere."

I hadn't had time to give it much thought. "I'll discuss it with the Sergeant. At the moment, he's under-staffed and seems intent on pinning the crime on O'Malley, dead or alive. It's odd he's not interrogating other suspects. Locating the stolen horses is probably not on his radar, yet. That could work to our advantage in finding them first. A starting point, at this end, might be for me to talk to the breeder-seller of the missing animals – he's supposed to live nearby."

Simon hesitated. I could almost hear his mind churning. "I'll be home tomorrow. Why don't I call Kit," he said, "and bring her up to date? We need to be straightforward about the reward thing. Then I'll do some research on the Farrells. If I'm not mistaken, that's a big name in horse show circles."

"Call me from the U.S. as soon as you're settled," I said.

"I'll do that." Simon paused. "By the way, I miss you."

"How could you? You've been busy with Emma."

"I'll tell all in time. Sleep well, P.J. I'm not sure I'll enjoy working with you long distance."

"It's not forever. Goodnight, Simon – I miss you, too."

6

Despite the luxurious king-size bed, I didn't sleep well. Maybe I was concerned that Clancy might come calling again. In any case, I was up and dressed before dawn and decided to throw on a sweater and take a stroll around the grounds. The night manager, Frank Reilly, was reading at a desk off the entrance hall, in full view of the carpeted staircase. He suggested I first circle the manor for an appreciation of the size of the estate.

From the front steps, in the early morning mist, I could barely see the herd of horses on the other side of the ditch – some grazing, a few snoozing under a tree. Then there was Clancy. You couldn't miss him, even at daybreak. He was so big and colorful, standing alone on the brink of the trench, watching my every move. I suppose he was considering whether to jump across and risk another scolding.

I walked across the lawn, about fifty yards wide, to the edge of the bar ditch. It ran for nearly a hundred yards and was joined at both ends by standard fencing that enclosed the pasture. The channel was approximately eight feet wide by five feet deep and half full of water. Clancy had to be one courageous horse to leap across without the encouragement of a rider's whip. I also thought, he would provide some stout rider many great days in the hunt field.

When I'd driven into St. Clerans the night before, I'd crossed a narrow bridge over a stream that spilled into a tranquil pool. Overhanging trees and a variety of shrubs lined the banks of this peaceful setting. This morning I wanted to take a closer look and followed a path around the side of the hotel. As I approached the bridge, I noticed a shadowy figure in an outback hat, who appeared to be fishing. He didn't seem to notice me so rather than startle him, I stopped and said, "Good morning. Having any luck?"

He flinched, half-turned and began rapidly reeling in his line. He was a husky man in a wax cotton jacket and Wellington boots. Without saying a word, he picked up his gear and jogged off in the opposite direction. And I thought all Irishmen were supposed to be friendly. In the half light, this encounter gave me an eerie feeling so I abandoned my walk and returned to the manor for breakfast.

Mr. Reilly was still at his desk.

"I ran into a man fishing off the bridge," I said. "I don't think he's a guest. Who could he be? We seem so far from everything."

He hesitated. "He's probably just a poacher from

Craughwell, the nearest village. They know this is private land, but once in a while someone can't resist a trout meal. The fishing is good under the bridge."

I had the feeling that Mr. Reilly was holding something back, that he'd told me just another fishing yarn.

I ordered the Complete Irish Breakfast – juice, two eggs up, ham, chunky potatoes, muffins with honey and a side of kippered herring. Herring was new to me but not half bad.

Sergeant McConnell had suggested that as soon as I could *collect myself,* I should meet him at the Central Garda. He seemed surprised to find me on his doorstep when he arrived for work at 8:15 a.m. "I hope you haven't been here all night," he quipped.

"No, but I might as well have." Then I told him about my introduction to Clarence. I was tempted to also mention my encounter with the mysterious fisherman, but I let that pass.

"I know Clarence," he said. "He's a character, but no question, one of the great hunt horses in Galway. He's owned by St. Clerans, and guests reserve him months in advance. Do you foxhunt?"

"I did in England – my first time. It was exciting, and I'm proud to say, I never fell off!"

"Well, good for you! But with the ban and all, they really don't hunt over there. If you want to ride in a real chase, Ireland's the place. And the Galway Blazers is the most celebrated club in the world. Still, 'tis not for the faint of heart. If you're up to it, maybe we can go out together some morning."

Officer McConnell was making a move on me. He probably knew the Irish brogue cast a spell over naïve American girls. "We'll see. I don't know how much time I'll have. When are we going to the Cliffs of Moher?"

He smiled. "Ah, Margaret will be here any minute, then we can be on our way."

The drive along the ocean was spectacular. It was different from our West Coast – no sandy beaches – just waves crashing over stones and boulders. Most of the shoreline was steep rocky bluffs facing the white-capped Atlantic. And through the mist I could make out the primitive Aran Islands – Inishmore, Inishmaan and Inisheer – accessible only by ferry or small plane. I'd been told the total population was about one thousand five hundred with the main occupation being tourism.

The Cliffs of Moher were a jagged promontory that was higher and steeper than the rest of the coast. McConnell, in an official blue jumpsuit and billed hat, lead us through the guardrail toward the edge where O'Malley had allegedly leapt to his death. The wind howled off the ocean as we walked to the brink. I buttoned my jean jacket and pulled down my cap. Dark clouds on the horizon signaled that a storm could be rolling in from the west.

"How do you know he jumped here?" I asked, leaning into the wind.

McConnell nodded toward where we had parked.

"His truck was abandoned in that lot." Then he pointed straight down. "We retrieved a tweed cap with a wire line, about a hundred feet below. It was identified as his. The evidence is circumstantial but convincing."

"I guess so." It seemed staged to me. Why bounce off seven hundred feet of flesh-tearing rocks when you could just as easily put a gun to your head? I would have taken the quicker way out. But these cliffs were a national treasure, and O'Malley might have aspired to make a sensational exit.

Again, McConnell motioned toward the bottom of the cliff where the sea crashed and foamed into crevices and over craggy peaks. "You can see why we've not recovered the body. The undertow is formidable."

At that moment another police vehicle pulled into the parking lot. "Here's Warden Paddy Nolan," McConnell said as he walked over to greet him. I followed.

Nolan was a tall, thin man with a pale, pock-marked complexion, long, slender jaw and a nose that looked like it'd been in too many pub brawls. He wore a soiled, olive-colored uniform with black piping on his sleeves and cap.

McConnell introduced us. "Anything new on the body, Paddy?"

"Nothing, yet, sir. Two more men with high powered binoculars will be here in a bit, and if the weather holds, we'll drive south and scour the coastline. And there's a washed out cavern down there to the right we'll have to check – maybe by boat."

McConnell nodded. "What are the chances the current swept the body out to sea?"

"That's possible," Nolan replied, adjusting his cap, "but when debris falls in, it normally works its way along the bank. A body might do the same."

"And no shreds of clothing, other than the cap, were ever spotted?" I asked.

"That's all, miss."

McConnell asked, "Any other questions, P.J.?"

I wasn't convinced that anyone would jump off this scary ledge. "Do many people end their lives here, Warden?"

"Five jumpers last year alone, miss."

My cynicism dissolved.

The wind stiffened, pelting us with rain. My jacket wasn't waterproof. McConnell studied the darkening horizon. "A storm's on the way. Why don't we drive up the coast a couple of miles and have a bite to eat at Crag House? 'Tis on an adjacent promontory with a good view of Moher and the ocean."

"Sounds nice."

In the states, Crag House would have been constructed of logs and stone for the sake of charm. Here, it was white-washed concrete block. Could be a shortage of oversize timber in Ireland, or maybe they preferred the simplicity and cost-saving of cement.

The ocean side of the restaurant was all glass, providing the panoramic view McConnell had promised.

He led me through a sliding door onto a crescent, railed veranda which seemed dangerously close to the edge. If the Cliffs of Moher were seven hundred feet high, this was probably six hundred.

A telescope was mounted near the brink for guests to scan the Aran Islands and check for passing ships. Though the rain and mist shrouded the land, I asked, "May I take a look?"

"Ah, you're welcome to try."

Though the spyglass was powerful, I could barely make out the islands. No ships were in sight. The ocean was furious with ten to twenty foot swells. Finally, I studied the Cliffs of Moher – steep, saw-toothed and treeless. I swept down the slope to the base, focused and re-focused. A spot of color was visible along the surf. As I studied it further, I couldn't believe my eyes. "Ross, come here! Take a look at this!"

I steadied the telescope as he peered into the eyepiece. He pulled back, shaking his head. "God, P. J., it looks like a body! Is that what you see?"

"Yes! It must be O'Malley!"

7

McConnell and I skipped lunch to race back to Galway City. As soon as we hit the highway, heading north, he notified Warden Nolan about the corpse, then called his office.

He had Margaret inform his entire staff of our discovery. "Anyone on leave is to report for duty, first thing in the morning," he snapped. "No excuses!"

I recalled yesterday, when two of McConnell's men had reported in sick but were suspected of actually foxhunting. The mavericks were about to be roped in.

McConnell explained that the coastal patrol would attempt to recover the body by motorboat as soon as the weather relented, possibly tomorrow. Representatives from the Central Garda would be on hand to make a preliminary examination of the cadaver, then supervise its transfer to the Galway City Coroner.

"If the rough weather persists, is there any other way to retrieve the body?" I asked.

"It's too dangerous to go in on foot or by helicopter. The cliff plunges straight down to the sea, and the updrafts are unbelievable. As a last resort, we can drop a team down the face, but that's also treacherous, and it might disturb the stability of the cliffs which would involve reams of government red tape."

"Meanwhile you're losing valuable evidence."

He nodded.

While we drove in silence, watching the wind and rain whip across the road and jostle our small car, I considered how to occupy my time until the coastal patrol salvaged the remains. An idea popped into my head. "Ross, I'd like to talk to the man who bred and sold the missing horses to O'Malley. Could that be arranged?"

He looked askance and smiled. "Ah, that might take some doing."

"Sounds like it's going to cost me," I joked.

Stroking his chin, he said, "Not much atall, miss."

I shifted in my seat. "What'd you have in mind?" I asked.

"If you'd invite me for dinner tonight at St. Clerans, I'd pay my part."

"Seems fair." Truth was I welcomed the company. Not only was McConnell physically appealing, I'd enjoy comparing law enforcement backgrounds. More importantly, he might be useful in locating the stolen horses.

"You've got a deal," I added, extending my hand.

With a single squeeze, he sealed the bargain. "I'll be busy this afternoon, still I'll make time to call Jimmy Craigh and arrange for you to meet with him tomorrow. He lives only five miles from your hotel, but the roads twist and turn. I'll draw a map and give it to you tonight. And I'll give you my cell number in case you get lost, but a smart, comely lass like yourself should have no trouble atall."

I paused to consider the downside of having dinner with this guy. He was a little pushy, but what could it hurt? It might even be fun. "I'll make a reservation for two at seven."

"I'll be there."

I smiled modestly. "We're talking just dinner, right?"

"Of course, m'lass. You've not a worry in the world."

I wondered.

* * * * * * *

When I returned to St. Clerans, Reilly was just going off duty. "Miss Porter, you received a call from Dr. Guy Porter in the States. Himself claimed to be your father. Number's in your key box. Wanted you to phone back as soon as you arrived."

"Did he say what it was about?"

"No, miss – just asked that you return his call promptly."

I requested that he make the dinner reservation for Ross and me.

The corners of his mouth formed a vague frown. What did he have against McConnell?

I also mentioned that I'd spent the day with Sergeant McConnell at the Cliffs of Moher, and we'd spotted what we believed was the body of Sean O'Malley. Reilly's face paled.

"O'Malley drowned! Impossible!" he blurted.

I was reminded of his peculiar expression when, early this morning, I mentioned that I'd encountered that jittery fisherman. "What's going on, Mr. Reilly? Do you know something that the police don't?"

He only gave me a worried look, then turned and disappeared through a door labeled *Private*.

Back in my room, I threw my jacket and ball cap on the bed and called my father. I thought it was odd he'd telephone me when he knew I'd be coming home in a few days.

"Hello, Dad. It's Parker," I said when he answered. I'd picked up the "P.J." in college, and it had stuck. But my mother and father still called me Parker. "Everything all right there?"

"Well, no, it isn't, I'm sorry to say."

I pulled up a chair. "What's wrong, Dad?"

I could hear my father catch his breath. "It's your horse, honey. Transport was bitten by a copperhead."

I gasped. "Oh, no! How awful! Is he dead?"

My father was a veterinarian and head of equine research at Oklahoma State's College of Veterinary Medicine.

"No, but it's been touch and go," he replied. "I had him picked up by the Vet Med staff and moved to Stillwater. He's getting the best care possible."

"I'm glad you called. Do you know where it happened?" Snakes had been known to wander into horse stalls, but it was extremely rare.

"Transport had spent the day in the pasture. When he didn't come in for his evening grain, the foreman went looking and found him down by the stream. Transport's left front leg was swollen about the size of an elephant's, and he was in shock with severe tremors. The crushed snake was ten feet away. After it bit him, Transport must have panicked and stomped it to death. Knowing it was a copperhead was helpful – Vet Med knew which anti-venom to inject."

"Where was the bite?" I asked.

"Just above the hoof, on the pastern. The problem is your horse was out too long before we learned what happened. Frightened and in pain, there was no way he could make his way back to the barn on his own."

My body sagged. Why was I here when I was needed at home? The reward money wasn't that important. Of course, I knew the real reason – the soft spot in my heart for Kit Devereux and for all the pain and embarrassment inflicted on her by her outrageous mother, Barbara. Now that should be Kit's problem. Mine was Transport!

I gathered my wits. "What's his prognosis" I asked.

"Can't be sure. Dr. Mason Jett, the toxicologist,

is in charge and has him on antibiotics and painkillers. Transport's temperature is still very high. Dr. Jett also has him suspended in a sling to take the weight off his legs and prevent founder. I'm sorry, honey, but we'll just have to wait and see."

"Should I come home?" I asked. I could be there by late tomorrow.

"That's up to you, Parker. But there's nothing you can do. However, I'd like your permission to put him down if he relapses into shock. There'd be no reason to prolong his misery."

"Oh, Dad, I can't give you that authority. He's my first horse – my love. We grew up together. If it comes to that, I'll drop everything and fly home. I don't want him euthanized without me being there! Do you understand?"

"I do, Parker. And I give you my word."

"Please call me immediately, if there's any change. Meanwhile, I'll try to wind things up. And, Dad, thanks for everything! I'll be praying."

I grabbed a tissue from the bedside table and dabbed my eyes and mopped my nose. Why had fate detoured me to this unfamiliar, rain-swept land? There'd better be a good reason for me to stay, or I was out of here!

8

When I was seven, attending Chandler Elementary, I rode my bicycle to and from school – a two mile trek. Roadside attacks or kidnappings were unheard of in rural Oklahoma at that time. Even doors were left unlocked. Now things were different.

Every day I passed Mayor William Rodgers' tidy green and white frame house with attached barn, located on ten acres at the edge of town. His property was enclosed by a post and rail fence which usually contained a grazing horse or two. The animals were so accustomed to seeing me pedaling by, and so intent on enjoying the lush grasses, that they seldom even raised their heads.

One day, I spotted a small addition to the tiny herd – a leggy, blood chestnut foal with a bolt of white lightning running down his face and two white socks. I guessed he was less than a month old and cute as could be. As soon as he noticed me, he hopped away from the dam and began trailing me along the rail. This was unusual because foals rarely leave their mothers to approach humans. They're too busy bonding and are intimidated by unfamiliar people, noises and surroundings.

I lingered next to the fence and extended my hand. "Hi, pretty boy. Come here and say hello," I said. He stopped, cocked his head and stared at me. His deep chestnut coloring and white markings were striking, and he looked at me with the most doleful, trusting eyes I'd ever seen. "Okay, I understand. I'll see you tomorrow." I waved goodbye and pedaled off.

For the next year, he was always waiting when I rode by, probably because I brought him treats like sugar cubes or bits of carrots. That winter, when I came down with the flu, old Mayor Rodgers called my parents to see how I was. Pretty Boy had not been eating and, night after night, had been pacing in his stall. When I recovered and resumed biking to school, the colt's temperament had become more demanding. He would prance with excitement when I appeared and became agitated, shaking his head, when I said goodbye. And, if I'd forgotten his treat, there was hell to pay!

Then one fall day, when he was about two, our relationship changed forever. I was riding home, searching the pasture for Pretty Boy, but there was no sign of him. I figured he was locked in his stall, maybe ill or injured. Suddenly, he burst open the barn door, charged toward me in a panic and, with the graceful leap of a gazelle, vaulted the four foot fence, landing softly nearby. He trotted up and began nuzzling my hand as if nothing unusual had happened, begging for food and attention. I moved alongside, looped my arms around his neck, then hugged him and sighed, "Oh, Pretty Boy. You're something." Rather than jump away in fear, which young horses do when embraced, he moved closer and rubbed his head against my chest and whinnied. My heart skipped a beat. I'd never been moved like this by an animal. *Where was this relationship going?*

I had to escort him back to his enclosed pasture. Climbing on my bike, I motioned Pretty Boy to follow and pedaled along the shoulder to the driveway leading to the Rodgers' home. The colt didn't hesitate to fall in line behind me. Mr. Rodgers was on his front porch, looking aggravated, when we arrived. "I saw that from the window," he barked. "It's lucky he didn't break his fool neck jumping that big fence. He's never done anything like that before."

"No, sir, I don't think he has."

The mayor's expression was stern. "Parker, I've watched you with that horse. You've been feeding and petting him like he was yours. The problem is he's bonded with you rather than his mother or anyone here at the farm. He'll not be much good to us. I'm afraid you're going to have to buy him."

I dropped my bike. "Oh! Mr. Rodgers, I'm sorry if I've caused a problem. Of course I'd like to buy him, but my father couldn't afford a beautiful horse like this."

The mayor held up his hand. "Now, hold on, young

lady! You haven't heard my price!"

It had never occurred to me that I could own such an animal. "What would you want for him?"

"Well, let's see. He's a registered Quarter Horse, excellent breeding and the promise of being a great mover. And you know he'll be a super jumper! We've seen that! There's a man in Ft. Worth who's offered me twenty-five thousand before he's even broke to the saddle."

"Oh, Mr. Rodgers, we couldn't afford anything like that," I exclaimed.

"Well, just a minute, missy! Since he seems to want to belong to you anyway, and I know you'd take good care of him, what would you think of....say....a thousand dollars?"

My jaw dropped. "Goodness, Mr. Rodgers. You sure? That's wonderful! Please don't sell him to anyone else till I ask my father."

I jumped on my bike and tore for home. I prayed that dad would not be mad at me for interfering. As it turned out, he thought a thousand dollars was a bargain and was as excited as I was.

By the time Pretty Boy, registered name *Transport to Glory*, was four, we'd blue-ribboned in every Hunter Class I could find to enter. When he was six, at the National Quarter Horse Show in Oklahoma City, he was crowned Super Horse of the Year.

That was just the start of his spectacular career.

Now Transport was seventeen, with more triumphs ahead in the sport of Eventing. Sadly though, he now hovered on the verge of an excruciating, venomous death. And here I was, four thousand miles away and helpless to comfort him. Loving an animal can be so damned painful!

9

McConnell was on time, looking like a Ralph Lauren model in navy jacket, soft green turtleneck and white flannel trousers – unusually stylish for a police officer, I thought. His wavy, black hair had been carefully arranged to affect a windblown look. Ross cut a handsome figure, but I couldn't help wondering if he could be trusted. There was something about him, maybe the perfect hair, that signaled *proceed with caution*.

Compared to his sartorial elegance, I was embarrassed by the same tired threads I'd worn for every dressy occasion in England – black slacks, colorful silk blouse, charcoal cashmere sweater thrown over the shoulders, and artificial pearls. Of course, no handbag. After I'd become a police officer, I rarely carried a purse. If I needed money, credit card, driver's license or lipstick, I relied on pockets or a money belt.

"Shall we stop in the bar first?" Ross asked, grinning and rubbing his hands together.

I wasn't interested in making a long night of it. "It's almost seven. We can have a drink at the table."

He frowned but nodded.

Strolling toward the dining room, he said, "You're a bonnie lass, P.J. I don't know any female officer in Galway, or anywhere in Ireland for that matter, that looks as good as you. Truth is – we don't have many ladies in service over here, but that's still a compliment."

"Thank you, sir. You look pretty snappy yourself." I was tempted to apologize for my wrinkled attire, but he was probably so caught up in his own appearance that he hadn't really noticed mine.

The off-white, pictureless dining room was warmed with salmon-colored drapes and classic carved molding that edged the oval ceiling. A palatial Venetian chandelier hung from the center. As we waited to be seated, I counted eight tables of varying sizes around the perimeter of the room. A round serving platform stood in the center. All were covered with starched linen and decorated with porcelain vases containing fresh flowers.

Once we were seated, McConnell asked, "Why don't we share a bottle of wine?"

"Good idea. What do you suggest?"

"I'm sure they stock Kermit Lynch. Sounds Irish, which makes it popular here, but it's actually French. It's an excellent Rhone and fairly priced. We'll split the dinner, but the wine's on me."

"In that case, I'd love to try the Kermit Lynch."

As I was toying with the Francis the First silverware, a well-endowed waitress, whose white uniform should have been at least a size larger, came up to McConnell and lightly brushed her hip against him. She looked down with a mischievous grin. "Well now, Ross me boy, can I bring you and your friend something to drink?"

McConnell's face flushed. "Hello, Fiona. I didn't know you were on staff here. When did you start?"

"This is my second week. When did you begin eating here, so high and mighty?" She quickly glanced at me to check my reaction.

He shifted in his chair. "It's my first time at St. Clerans. Fiona, girl, would you please bring us a bottle of the Kermit Lynch Rhone?"

"Yes, *sir*," she mocked and marched toward the bar, flipping her hair back as she went.

McConnell fidgeted with his hands on the table and looked around the room, studying the ceiling and the other guests. The room was about two thirds full of chattering customers. If he was waiting for me to inquire about Fiona, I wasn't about to show any interest.

Instead, I asked, "Did you bring the map to Jimmy Craigh's farm?"

"I did." He reached into his coat pocket and withdrew a folded piece of paper. "Aren't you going to ask about Fiona McBride?"

"It's none of my business."

"Right, I know that, but I want to clear the air.

Fiona's from Limerick. When she first came to Galway City, about a year ago, she worked at Blarney Spoken Here. We had a few dates, but that's the extent of it. We're just friends."

He waited for my reaction, expecting me to be relieved and understanding. How arrogant of him to assume I cared at all! "I believe you," I said, glancing away.

It was obvious Fiona had a chip on her shoulder. Their relationship, whatever it was, might be over for him, but it wasn't for her. Anyway, I felt it was important for me to appear indifferent. I wanted our relationship friendly but kept at arms' length.

A lull in the conversation followed. Then I noticed Mr. Reilly, the grim-faced night manager, standing at the doorway, staring. He seemed like an odd person. Why was he so curious about us?

"May I see the directions?" I asked, anxious to get back on track.

Ross hesitated, then unfolded the map. I examined the route and realized that without it, Craigh's farm would be nearly impossible for me to find. There were six or more turns and forks in the road, each noted by a local landmark: *left at the fallen oak* and *right at the old rock barn*.

Fiona returned with the wine.

Ross took a sip, rolled it around in his mouth as if he were a connoisseur, then smiled. "It's a bonnie vintage. Miss McBride, if you see Mr. Lynch, tell him I approve."

"Ah, I'll do that, sir," she said, then poured me a glass,

spilling a few drops on the immaculate tablecloth. Was that intentional? Fiona had been building up a head of steam, and if I were not there, she might have given Ross a piece of her mind.

As she passed menus, I continued to study the sketch. Once she'd moved on to attend to other guests, I said, "Thank you for drawing this, Ross. Without it, finding Craigh's farm would be tricky. It's certainly worth a dinner invitation."

McConnell laughed – deep and husky. "You're set for tomorrow then. Jimmy Craigh will be working around the barn or his arena all morning. You can arrive any time before noon. Be careful though. Since you're American, I'm sure he'll try to sell you a horse."

"Thanks. I appreciate the heads up. But I can't afford another horse. Two's enough."

"What's their breeding?"

"Transport, my old horse, is a Quarter Horse, and Cargo, my new baby, a future eventer, is a husky Thoroughbred–Shire cross."

I was about to mention that Transport could be on the verge of death, then changed my mind. It was too depressing. Besides, since St. Patrick had expelled all vipers from the Emerald Isle, the Irish had no appreciation of the lethal effect of a snake bite on a horse.

"Shire is an English draft – goes back to the Norman Conquest," Ross said. "Would you like to see some beautiful Irish Draft horses while you're here?"

"Sure. When?"

"Actually, tomorrow afternoon at Kilcolgan would be a good time. There's a show – not far from here. Assuming O'Malley's body is not yet recovered, I'll be presenting one of my own."

Before I could answer, Fiona interrupted to take our dinner orders. She was clearly intent on interfering with the enjoyment of our meal. But despite whatever had occurred between them, Ross was not about to be rushed or flustered – not on his first, long awaited dinner at St. Clerans.

"Fiona, allow us a few more minutes, would you please?" he asked calmly.

"Certainly, *sir!*" She swished off.

The menu appeared to be mostly French without translation or prices. When the waitress returned I ordered item two – *Honey Roasted Breast of Barbary Duck with Orange Contreau Sauce*, while Ross, after much indecision, finally selected number four – *Grilled Fillet of Slaney Valley Beef with Sauce Poivrade and Wild Rice Pilaff with Melted Cashel Blue Cheese*. Kit would be shocked when she received my bill. I'd simply explain there'd been no dining alternative. Would she buy that? Would she even care?

We skipped the appetizer but were each served a small dish of *Champignons en Croute* with a flute of champagne – "compliments of the house." These mushrooms in pastry were delicious, more unusual than anything I'd eaten in England, and the bubbly was a lovely touch.

I leaned back in my chair, pleased with the five-star treatment. "I've never heard of a draft horse show," I said. "What's involved?"

"There are a few hunter classes, and it's amazing how agile those big fellows are over fences. But the main events are conformation, shown by the owners or professional handlers with the horses on leads. They're presented at different paces around a hundred meter circle. And following the show, you'll see something uniquely Irish – the lively buying and selling of some of those loveable giants. P.J., I know you'd enjoy it."

"I'm anxious to see it. Can I just meet you there after my trip to Craigh's farm?"

"That'd be fine, since I'll be busy primping Herbie. Herbie's my two thousand pound dumpling that I'll be showing.

"Check your Galway road map. When you arrive at the center square in Kilcolgan, just ask for directions to the Irish Draft Show on Kilcolgan Down. Competition will start around two in the afternoon and last 'til dark."

"Sounds easy." He was certainly keeping me entertained. I appreciated it – for now.

He smiled and his shoulders relaxed some, maybe deciding that Fiona could be pacified later. "Ah, you're welcome. 'Tis my pleasure," he said. "If you don't mind me saying, I'd like to spend more time with you."

I wasn't sure how to respond. Ross McConnell was *a fine cut of a man* with a charming accent, but I had two problems – First, I would be returning to the U.S. in a few days, and the second was my business associate and potential love-interest, John Simon Rush. "Ross, I'd like that, but remember, I may be going home at any time."

"Maybe I can persuade you to stay awhile."

I hesitated, then replied with a coy grin.

While I had reservations about Ross McConnell, I recalled my feelings toward Simon when we first met. Simon had spine-tingling physical appeal but was a suspected murderer. I mistrusted him completely, but this changed in a mere two days. I shouldn't write off Ross McConnell too quickly.

The dinner was superb, and despite Fiona's hovering, Ross kept me entertained with stories of growing up in Cork and finding his way into law enforcement. In turn, I intrigued him with a bit of my heritage – my mother was one-quarter Cherokee Indian and a descendant of Sequoyah, the creator of the Cherokee alphabet. I admitted to Ross that when we'd first met, I thought he might be part Indian, with his thick black hair, fair complexion and prominent check bones. He explained that he had no such blood but was considered Black Irish – a mixture of Irish and Spanish blood dating from the time of the Spanish Armada in 1588 when many shipwrecked Spanish sailors were washed up on the Irish coastline and had stayed.

We also discussed the case against Sean O'Malley which struck me as thin. The investigation seemed tabled until the body we spotted at the Cliffs of Moher was recovered. I was surprised that McConnell and the Central Garda in the meantime were not pursuing any other leads or suspects. They seemed convinced that O'Malley was the culprit and supporting evidence would be collected once the corpse had been recovered from the ocean. I questioned what physical evidence would remain after the body had fallen seven hundred feet, glancing off jagged rocks, then buffeted by the angry sea over razor-sharp reefs, not to mention a possible shark feeding frenzy. But none of this seemed to matter.

From the tone of McConnell's voice and his indifferent manner, I suspected he bore a grudge against O'Malley which might have closed his mind to other possibilities. If I were in charge, I'd examine their relationship. And I'd bet a woman was involved, maybe Fiona.

Once Ross and I had finished our meal, signed separate checks and were strolling toward the hotel lobby, I extended my hand. "Ross, I had a wonderful evening. The food was outstanding, and so was the company."

He took my hand. "I couldn't have said it better meself. Maybe we'll have time for a pint and a bite to eat at Kilcolgan."

Before I could offer an excuse, we were interrupted by a gray haired woman, wearing *pince-nez* glasses and an ill-fitting tweed suit. "Miss, there's a long distance call holding for you in the office."

"For me?" I asked. "Who is it?"

"I couldn't say. 'Twas Mr. Reilly accepted it."

I glanced at Ross. "It's probably my American friends, anxious for an update. This might take a while. If you don't mind, I'll say goodnight and see you tomorrow."

He half smiled, shook my hand and marched out. Now I had a new problem – soothing hurt masculine feelings. But I had had some experience with this.

As I followed the woman into the office I was confronted by Mr. Reilly, who ushered me into his private quarters. Closing the door and without inviting me to sit, he said, "There's no phone call, Miss Porter. I'm just relaying a message from a friend who'd like to meet with you."

I looked around the room. "Who?"

"Sean O'Malley."

I grasped the back of a chair. "I don't understand. He's supposed to be dead!"

"Not atall, miss. He's very much alive. He's been living in the Huston Cottage – behind the gated wall."

"I thought he drowned?"

"That was contrived....to give him a chance to prove his innocence. Will you meet with him, miss?"

"When?"

Reilly removed his glasses and squinted. "Tonight – at midnight – on the bridge where you saw him fishing this early morning."

"Oh, my God! That was O'Malley?"

10

I returned to my room with two and a half hours to kill. A million things ran through my mind. The foremost was, would I be safe meeting O'Malley on a bridge alone and in the middle of the night? I wish I had my trusty Glock 17 that I'd left behind with the Oklahoma City Police Chief. Maybe I should call Sergeant McConnell? No. If I did that, O'Malley would be locked up, and I might never hear his side of the story. What if I called Kit or her mother? Or Simon? Someone other than that strange night manager should be told what was going on. Oh, don't be chicken, I thought. I could handle myself – a black belt in karate. If O'Malley was alive – and innocent – I might be able to help him and the Devereuxs.

I changed into my jeans and warm jersey, set the alarm for 11:45 p.m., lay down on the bed and stared at the ceiling. Finally, I picked up a pamphlet from my bedside table, entitled "Anjelica's Story," and began to read:

Anjelica Huston is the daughter of the motion picture giant, director John Huston and Enrica Huston nee Soma. Anjelica was born while her father was working on the film The African Queen, *in 1951. She was the second child born to John and Enrica; her brother, Walter Anthony, was born in 1950. John Huston visited Ireland for the first time in 1951, and developed a great love for the country. By 1953, the Huston family had moved to Ireland. One day while riding with the Galway hunt, Huston saw St. Clerans for the first time. After visiting the old manor house, he became so enthralled that he set about purchasing it from the Irish Land Commission. Although it was a serious financial undertaking, Huston never regretted the cost of restoration work and declared that he had spent eighteen glorious years at St. Clerans ....*

When my alarm sounded, it took a few seconds for my mind to snap back. Anjelica's unusual childhood could wait. Dashing my face with cold water, slipping on my boots and jean jacket, tying my hair in the back and adjusting my ball cap, I was ready. Reilly was still on duty. As I passed his desk, he glanced up, nodded and resumed reading. I eased open the big front door and stepped under the dimly lit porte-cochere. Even the horses across the bar ditch were hidden behind a curtain of mist and darkness.

I let my eyes adjust to the night, then wound my way along the damp, shrub-lined path toward the bridge. The moon darted above the clouds and fog, supplying just enough light for me to stay on track. In minutes, the noise of the rushing stream signaled that I was near the bridge. I slowed my pace and peered across to where I'd seen the fisherman the previous morning. No one was there. Squinting to make sure, I looked around, searching for some movement in the gloom. I was alone and vulnerable in the dark. An overwhelming impulse to turn and run for the safety of the manor house swept over me.

However, at that moment, out of the shadows and dense foliage to my left, came the specter of a man. My knees buckled.

"Miss Porter," he whispered, "I'm Sean O'Malley."

I staggered back, trying to regain my balance.

He stood motionless. "Don't be frightened. I'm a friend of Barbara and Kit Devereux."

I clenched my fists. "My God, man, don't do that to me!" I exclaimed.

"Ah, I'm sorry. I had to make sure you were alone. Are you all right?"

I willed my heartbeat to slow. "Yes, I think so." It took a moment longer for the initial scare to be replaced by irritation. "Now what's this all about?" I growled.

"I just want to explain what's happened so you can relay it to the Devereuxs."

I braced my hands on my hips. "Mr. O'Malley, if it's really you, everyone thinks you're dead! And why meet in the middle of the night and scare me half to death?"

"I'm Sean O'Malley himself, for sure, alive but in

trouble. Again, I'm sorry for the fright. But you must believe I had nothing to do with the theft of those horses, and I don't know who did. And please keep this to yourself – Frank Reilly is my cousin. He's allowed me to hide in the Huston cottage." He pointed toward the ivy covered wall with an iron gate, behind the hotel. "'Tis in that courtyard – been closed for years. I'm there 'til I find out what's going on."

The anxiety in his voice made me fairly confident this man was indeed O'Malley – or a clever actor.

"How do you plan to learn anything when you can only come out at night?" I asked. "And you'll have a bigger problem when the police retrieve that body floating in the ocean near the Cliffs of Moher. They're convinced it's you."

His head jerked up. "What are you talking about? What body?"

"You haven't heard? It still hasn't been recovered, but when it is, you may also be charged with homicide."

O'Malley shook his head and ran his fingers through his hair. "No. I hadn't heard that. But I promise you, I had nothing to do with it."

He hesitated as if considering his dilemma. "Miss Porter, this body thing is all the more reason I need assistance. I've heard you're a clever detective," he said. "I'm hoping you can help me."

"Clever, my eye! I'm an American police officer, with limited experience. And I'm on leave – anxious to get home. All I've heard is that you're accused of fleecing people by the name of Farrell, out of two, very valuable show jumpers. How in the world could I help? And even if I could, why should I?"

He glanced toward the bank of the stream. "Please. There's a bench over there. Let's sit down, and I'll tell you what I know."

The ominous sounds of cascading water and rustling trees made me hesitate.

"Please, miss," he pleaded.

As we ambled across the bridge, I studied O'Malley. He was tall and broad shouldered, probably mid-forties, with weathered good looks. It didn't take much to figure out why Barbara Devereux had yielded to a tumble in the hay.

Still, I was uneasy sitting alone with this suspected horse thief and possible murderer. "Okay, what's this all about?" I blurted impatiently.

He rubbed his hands together. "Six weeks ago, I received a telephone call from Tex Farrell. His family is prominent on the American hunter-jumper circuit. His daughter, Maureen, is a professional rider and trainer. They were looking for a couple of young Irish Sport Horses with promising show records. I'd been recommended as an agent by the Devereuxs and other Texas clients. I told Farrell I knew of some prospects that might work and would get back to him in a few days. That's how this whole mess started."

O'Malley sighed, leaned back on the bench and

continued. He knew a local breeder, Jimmy Craigh, who might have what the Farrells were looking for – two five-year-olds, sired by a renowned Irish Draft, Murphy Himself, out of different Thoroughbred mares with credible breeding. They'd already established impressive records at the Royal Dublin and Millstreet shows, as well as Hickstead in England. When O'Malley went to Craigh's farm, he was so certain the horses would be perfect for the Farrells, he videoed them on the spot.

Once the Farrells had seen the film, reviewed their show records and approved a veterinary exam, an agreement was struck.

Just then, there was a startling splash in the pool below us. O'Malley sprang to his feet and held a finger to his lips as he looked around. Finally, he sat back down. "'Tis probably a trout – and here we are without our rods."

I was not amused. "What happened after the Farrells agreed to buy the horses?"

"When the sale had been finalized and almost three million dollars had been wired to my account, the horses were picked up by the transport agent, Grady Quinn, for delivery to Shannon Airport, then on to the U.S. It was only after they'd reached Dallas that they were discovered to be frauds. The Farrells accused me."

"I'd be inclined to suspect you, too."

"Ah, but I didn't do it!"

"Don't you have friends or family who can help?" I asked.

"None atall! I was counting on Sergeant McConnell's support, but when I heard he also accused me, I figured I was done for. I staged my suicide at the cliffs and went into hiding. I knew I'd need time to clear my name. Now, they're going to think I killed whoever's floating in the ocean."

"Did you?"

"No! I swear I know nothing about that. With help, I can straighten this out. But I need you to do some leg work for me. P.J., I'm desperate."

"What kind of leg work?"

"For starters, I wish you'd talk to the people who sold and shipped the horses. When the body's retrieved from the ocean, there may be need for a different tack."

"O'Malley, I'll have to think about it." I saw no reason to mention that I'd already made arrangements to meet with Jimmy Craigh. "If McConnell believes I'm involved, in any way, he'll yank my passport, and I'll be stuck over here. But at least I can let the Devereuxs know what's going on."

"That's not good enough! You're the only one who can help me!"

"If I can, I will. But I warn you, I may be needed at home. I have to be ready to fly out at any moment....you better consider your options."

11

With McConnell's map on my lap, I headed for Jimmy Craigh's breeding farm. There were numerous twists and turns in the road without a single sign. I was told I'd recognize the entrance to his facility by stacked stone pillars on either side, but I missed the turn the first time because one column had toppled and was overgrown with lichen.

Jimmy Craigh was mucking out his modest, eight stall barn when I arrived. I was surprised the building was not more imposing. How could champion show jumpers be developed in a dirt-floored cowshed in need of paint and repair?

Standing at the barn door, I called, "Mr. Craigh, I'm P.J. Porter, friend of Sergeant McConnell. I hope I'm not intruding."

Throwing his pitchfork into a wheelbarrow, he said in a jolly voice, "Miss Porter, I've been expecting you. I'm pleased you found the place. You're not intruding atall.

And ye may call me Jimmy."

"I go by P.J."

Jimmy Craigh would have made the perfect Macy's Santa Claus – short, pudgy, ruddy complexion, bald on top with flowing white side burns. Removing his work gloves, he extended a small, calloused hand.

"Thank you for talking to me," I said. "I won't take up much of your time."

He chuckled. "Ah, time – I have nothing but. If I can help, I'd be pleased to. Let's go outside – I'll show you around."

The boundary of Craigh's property, which contained no more than twenty acres, was defined by the usual stacked stone walls. At the far end, on the highest point, stood his white stucco cottage. Laundry fluttered on a clothesline in front, with the remains of a rusting flatbed truck junked along the side.

We walked around to the back of the barn. Two fenced arenas were in use. These also needed paint and repair, and clumps of grass begged to be pulled. In one ring, a young man was schooling a beautiful black and white gelding over a series of four, tight jumps. In the second, a younger fellow, whip in hand, was exercising another flashy, colored horse on a lung line. The horses could have been a cloned pair.

Craigh motioned for me to sit in one of the dirty outdoor chairs scattered on top of a rise, overlooking the corrals. "We can watch and talk from here," he said.

Pointing, he added, "Those are my boys – Doyle, the one jumping, and the other is Toby. The coloreds are my latest prospects in training. I'm hoping they'll make good eventers."

"They look like winners to me. They must be related," I said.

"They're from the same sire, out of different dams – same type breeding program as the two horses the Farrell's bought."

"Where are the parents?" I asked. If Craigh was in the breeding business, there should be more horses running around. Also, I was curious about the size and color of the sire.

"I only do training and evaluation here, miss. I don't own enough land for much more. The two stallions and four mares I own are boarded at Willie Leahy's. He's the largest land owner and breeder around here."

That still didn't explain why his property wasn't better maintained, which bothered me. If this was where he demonstrated and videoed his stock for buyers, it should be more of a show place. But this was his problem, not mine.

I focused on the reason for my drive out. "O'Malley is why I'm here. Jimmy, if you don't mind, I'd like to ask you a few questions."

"Happy to tell you what I know," he said.

"Sergeant McConnell probably told you that I have friends in the U.S., the Devereuxs, who were associated with O'Malley in the show horse business. They don't believe he's the criminal type. They asked me to stop in Galway to inquire about the crime he's been accused of."

I was also anxious to size up Craigh. Though I could be wrong, he seemed an uncomplicated, content man – not the type to become involved in an elaborate scheme to steal his own horses. Besides, he had way too much to lose if he were even suspected, like his business and the possibility of alienating his sons.

"Jimmy, I know next to nothing about selling and exporting horses to the U.S. How would O'Malley arrange that?"

He nodded. "Sean O'Malley's an agent or broker – buys and sells horses for others. He knew I had two promising show jumpers in training – Rock of Cashel and Resident Magistrate. My son, Doyle, had competed with them in England and Ireland, and they showed world-class promise. O'Malley approached me on behalf of some wealthy American clients by the name of Farrell. We negotiated a deal, and in no time, the animals were off to the U.S."

"Was there any problem during the negotiations, like a money dispute?" I asked.

He shook his head. "None atall. The horses were sound, and the price was fair for the quality – just what the buyers were looking for."

At that moment something caught Jimmy's eye. "Sorry." He stood and called to his sons. "Doyle, that's enough jumping for one day. Jersey looks tired – he's nicking rails. Do ten minutes of flat work then put him up. Be sure and cover him with a cooler after you've hosed him down. The barn'll be chilly tonight."

"Hey, Toby!"

"Yeh, Pop."

"If you think Derry's settled down, set a Cavelletti course and work him under saddle for a half hour or so. That should be enough for today."

"Right, Pop."

Sitting down, Craigh told me that once he was paid, O'Malley had arranged for Grady Quinn, a local transport agent, to pick up the horses and deliver them to Shannon Airport. Before they were loaded, Quinn double checked the passports and took possession of them. These documents contained a record of the horses' size, color and unique markings, as well their birthdates and bloodlines. Quinn also electronically scanned the microchips that had been implanted in the horses' necks. Satisfied, he hauled the jumpers to Shannon and turned them over to the government inspector, Mr. Doyle Crouch. Crouch validated the passports before assigning the animals to flight containers for shipment. As far as Craigh knew, nothing was out of order prior to departing Ireland, and after investigating, the Central Garda had agreed.

From Shannon, the horses were flown nonstop to Kennedy International in New York and from there transported to the New York Animal Import Center at Rock Tavern, ninety miles up the Hudson, for testing and possible quarantine. Once they passed the medical exams, another independent driver picked them up and trucked them to the Farrells in Dallas.

Craigh leaned closer. "Here's the heart of it all. My horses set off with proper passports and microchips. Quinn and I confirmed this. But the bogus horses delivered to Dallas also arrived with passports and microchips that appeared to be valid – registered in the names of Resident Magistrate and Rock of Cashel. I don't know how that could have happened. Somewhere along the line a switch of horses, papers and microchips took place."

"I suppose passports could be forged by a pro," I said, "but how do you switch a tiny microchip, smaller than a pin head, imbedded in the neck muscle from one horse to another?"

Jimmy rubbed his head. "'Tis a good question. You'd have to cut into the animal's neck muscle. It would leave a nasty wound and risk muscle and nerve damage. You could ruin a million dollar prospect."

I nodded. "Jimmy, you've given me a lot to think about." I adjusted my ball cap. "I have one final question – where do you think the stolen horses could be?"

"If I had to guess, I'd say they were already in France or Germany – or maybe stashed in a remote barn, within a hundred miles of here, waiting to be flown abroad. That's the way it's been done before, and the thieves were never caught."

This was turning into a complicated case with limited

time to sort it out. As much as I hated to admit, I might need Simon's analytical mind to help brainstorm this thing.

12

Before joining Ross at Kilkolgan Down for the show, I returned to St. Clerans to freshen up and grab a sandwich. It was a blue-sky day, and the horses were bucking and romping in the field across the ditch. All except Clancy. For him it was another lazy afternoon for grazing. But when I climbed out of the car, he raised his head, studied me, whinnied, then trotted toward the edge of the trench. I walked over and extended my arm to greet him. Though he stretched his neck, the separation was too great for us to touch. He shook his head and nickered. Suddenly he leaped back and galloped away, then spun and charged in my direction. Nearing the brink of the moat, he slowed, coiled his long, powerful legs and propelled himself into the air, easily clearing the eight-foot trench and landing dangerously close to me.

I was momentarily stunned by the insistence of this leviathan to befriend me. "Clancy! Clancy!" I shouted, giving him a friendly slap on his muscular neck. "What in the world are you doing? You're going to be in serious trouble!"

Ignoring my warning, he reared up, vigorously pawing the air, as if to say to his pals on the opposite side: *look at me – free as a bird –come on over, the grass is greener.* Then he came down, pranced and neighed. What did he expect from me? I had no treats. I concluded this seventeen-plus-hand, brightly patterned giant was what the equestrian world referred to as *a character* – a horse that enjoyed interacting with humans and messing with their minds.

And why did these animals choose me to toy with? Did I smell of alfalfa? Or carrots? Something prompted them, first Transport, now Clancy, to leap fences and moats to be near me. Maybe it was my heritage – Indians have always possessed an uncanny rapport with horses.

Behind me I could hear O'Leary shouting, "Bad boy! Bad boy!" as he came running toward us with a rope. "You're going to kill yourself, Clancy! Lady Biddle-Jones will be furious if you're not fit to hunt tomorrow."

I stepped away as O'Leary looped the rope around Clancy's neck.

Stroking his long, broad back, I said, "Be nice to him. He just wanted attention."

"I will, miss. There's something about you he obviously likes. I've never seen him chase after a guest like that."

I was pleased that someone else recognized my

mystical power. "O'Leary, I heard Clancy is owned by the hotel. Does Lady what's-her-name rent him all the time?"

"Lady Biddle-Jones is from London, miss, and has him reserved for the hunt season," he replied. "But when she's unable to make it, the manor can assign him to someone else. You might inquire at the front desk.

"The hunt tomorrow will be special. It's the Blazers' 250th anniversary. The turnout will be huge."

As I climbed the stairs to the hotel entrance, I decided to check on Clancy's availability. What a high that would be to go bounding over the countryside on him, jumping walls and leaping off banks. We'd both enjoy the thrill of that.

However, before I could inquire, the receptionist handed me a note. "You received a call from a Dr. Mason Jett in the U.S.," she said. "He wants you to phone him back, any time of day."

"Thank you. Would you please have the kitchen deliver some small sandwiches and tea to my room?"

"Yes, miss. I'll take care of it immediately."

I hurried along the picture-lined corridor toward my suite. For the vet to call me, rather than my father, must mean something was wrong. I left my door ajar so lunch could be delivered and picked up the phone and dialed America. "Dr. Jett, this is P.J. Porter. How's Transport?"

"Parker, so glad you got my message."

In addition to my immediate family, everyone acquainted with me when I was young still called me Parker. But I'd grown used to P.J. in college and in my police work. The Chief preferred the initials – probably sounded more official.

"That's what I need to talk to you about," Dr. Jett said. "Transport's not any better – maybe worse. I'm concerned that he may have been in the pasture too long before we could treat him."

I slipped off my ball cap and grabbed a chair. "What can I do?"

"His temperature continues to be elevated, and his leg is still very swollen. This means the antibiotics and painkillers and anti-venom injections have not done their job. And despite an early tetanus shot, necrosis has set in around the snake bite, close to the pastern muscles. The flesh is turning black and will soon begin to slough. We can't let that continue. With your okay, I'd like to surgically clean it out."

"Doesn't that create new risks?"

"We do risk damaging the tendons. The thing is he's still suspended in a sling, and we've got to get him ambulatory to improve circulation. But to put any weight on that leg at this stage would cause terrific pain and trauma. I'm hoping surgery will remove the infection and reduce the swelling. That might enable him to take a few steps. But Parker, if surgery doesn't work, you must be prepared for the worst."

"When would you do the procedure?" I asked.

"Tomorrow or the day after, depending on his vitals."

I hesitated. "Dr. Jett, you have my permission to

perform the surgery and to use any medications you think will help. Please call me if there's the slightest change."

"I'll do that," he said and hung up.

Now I was really torn. Should I drop everything and fly home to console Transport? Still, there was my promise to the Devereuxs and the reward. Simon and I would need that money for law school. I was torn, but somewhere I'd heard – *when in doubt, stay the course.*

I was an only child, and when growing up, Transport had been my closest friend and constant companion. Knowing he would never reveal my secrets, I confided to him every youthful crisis and romantic disappointment. Now, the possibility of his imminent death, while I was three thousand miles away and helpless to comfort him, was heartbreaking.

As the maid arranged my lunch on the table next to me, I picked up the napkin and turned away to dab my eyes.

13

Kilcolgan was an easy, twenty minute drive south of St. Clerans.

Kilcolgan Down was a forty acre meadow on the outskirts. There were no buildings or grandstands, just a treeless pasture with a row of Porta-potties and three refreshment tents near the entrance.

Despite the bucolic setting, the area was teeming with talkers, gawkers, horse owners, trainers, grooms, buyers and officials. Unlike open-air horse shows in the U.S., there were no mink coats or designer boots – just waxed cottons, tweeds, Wellingtons and babushkas.

Two attendants, waiving yellow flags, directed traffic to the parking area – lorries and pickups towing horse trailers on one side and smaller vehicles, including numerous motorcycles and bicycles, on the other.

After locking the car, I headed toward the far end of the grounds where the conformation competition was in progress. My stroll was interrupted by a string of horses crossing my path on their way to various arenas. But it was a pleasure to step back and admire these gentle giants. Although Irish Drafts came in one size only – XXL – they were every shade of black, brown, grey and white and various combinations.

The modern Irish Draft in no way resembled the original beast of burden. It was still a horse of substance, usually around sixteen hands, but now, it was sleek and well-proportioned. Clancy was an Irish Draft. As a foxhunter, the breed was a popular choice of heavyweight riders, not only because drafts were strong and gentle, but because they were bold and careful jumpers when traversing open country. They were also reputed to be *bomb proof,* not easily spooked or rattled.

When crossed with the Thoroughbred, the Irish Draft produced the Irish Sport Horse, a superhorse. These were recognized as one of the most athletic hunters and show jumpers in the world, capable of leaping almost eight feet in a Puissance competition.

I passed one of the hunter rings where a jumping competition was in progress. The rails were set at just under four feet – not huge, but not low. This height was ideal for a potential buyer to see how each animal moved, changed leads, jumped and minded the aids of the rider. On average, Irish drafts weighed nearly a ton, and I was astonished at how gracefully they cantered and cleared the fences.

Studying the crowd, I was intrigued by a gathering of

men in countrified clothes, who appeared to be prospective buyers. They huddled together, speaking in accents so thick I could barely understand, and furtively discussing the merits of each horse as it passed. But it wasn't their attire or secretiveness that retained my attention, it was that most of them were puffing away on either pipes or cigarettes. And above the group hovered a gossamer halo of smoke — maybe symbolic of their future being cut short. Apparently they hadn't watched much American cancer-scare television.

Winding my way through the crowd, I neared the conformation arena. It was an oval track, enclosed by a single-strand rope fence. Approximately thirty Irish Drafts of every color were parading around the perimeter, led by their owners or trainers. Every animal looked as if it had been groomed in the same salon — manes and tails identically braided and every coat polished to an iridescent sheen.

Suddenly, there was angry shouting on the far side. I suspected a donnybrook might be in the making.

"Call an ambulance!" a woman screamed.

Someone else yelled, "Is there a doctor here?"

I grasped the arm of a towering spectator. "What's happened? Can you see?"

He looked down at me, adjusting his cap. "One of the horses charged into the crowd. Don't know why, miss. Must have trampled someone."

I elbowed my way to the rope. Though jostling

observers partially obstructed my view, it looked like two men were in each other's face, waving their arms and shouting obscenities.

The taller man cocked his fist and roared, "Don't you touch any of my horses, ever again!"

I sensed from the shouting and shoving that the crowd might be egging them on. But before any serious blows could be landed, three muscular men jumped in the middle of the fracas and brought it under control.

I leaned over the rope barrier to get a better look. I thought I recognized one of the fighters. I couldn't believe my eyes! It was my new friend – Sergeant Ross McConnell – the county peace officer.

14

"Loose horse! Loose horse!" someone cried. "Three down! Call an ambulance! Hurry!"

Another screamed, "It's Wexford! He's heading for the entrance! Stop him! Someone catch him!"

I imagined how lethal one of these frightened giants would be, plowing into an unsuspecting mob.

Backing away from the arena, I spotted the terror-stricken animal, racing along the perimeter of the show grounds, stumbling over his lead. If he continued on this course, Wexford would either charge through the front gate, maybe killing someone, or crash into the parked vehicles, seriously injuring himself.

I broke through the crowd and raced across the field to cut him off. I'd run the mile in college and was exhilarated by the challenge of outrunning a horse. Fortunately, Wexford slowed when he approached the chain-link barricade which turned him toward the parking lot. I beat him to the first row of trailers by seconds and raised my arms, waving wildly. I knew this could be dangerous because horses can be frightened by flailing arms and are known to run down the well-intentioned signaler.

Fortunately, Wexford slowed, looked around in wide-eyed confusion at the crowd pursuing him but stopped. I moved in close and grabbed his dangling lead.

Panting, I muttered, "Easy boy. You're fine." I stroked his forehead. "Relax, big fella. No one is going to hurt you." Gradually, he stopped prancing and settled down.

As I was guiding Wexford back to the arena, I was surrounded by observers, some patting me on the back, others shouting congratulations. Made me feel like I'd just won the Olympic Marathon.

Then a heavyset man in his mid-thirties, wearing a leather bomber jacket, sandy hair protruding from under a tweed cap, pushed through and motioned the crowd back. He grabbed my hand and shook it vigorously. "I'm Wexford's owner. Thank you, miss. Thank you. I didn't think anyone could catch him."

"I'm P.J.Porter — used to chasing animals around the farm in America."

"Ah well, you saved the day," he said. "And I know who you are. You're the lady staying at St. Clerans."

News traveled fast among country folk. "I hope the report's been favorable?" I asked.

"Oh, better than that, miss."

He reached for Wexford's lead. "Come on – walk with me to the trailer. Maybe we can figure out how to repay you."

We set out across the field for the parking area, dodging other horses being lead to and from the trailers and tiptoeing around and over countless horse deposits.

I'd begun to appreciate that most Irish men had rugged good looks and were courteous to the ladies. Nice combination.

"I'll walk with you, but you don't owe me a thing," I said. "I didn't want anyone, including the horse, to be harmed....By the way, what happened over there? Anyone hurt?" I asked, pointing toward the end of the arena where the ruckus had taken place.

"The ambulance rushed two men and a woman to the hospital. They were traumatized, I'm sure, but not seriously injured."

"How'd it happen?"

He hesitated. "I'm afraid it was my fault, miss. Wexford and I aggravated someone during the in-hand presentation. We were circling at the walk when the judges ordered contestants to trot. The team ahead of us was slow to pick up the stride which made everyone behind look sluggish. Irish Drafts are graded not only on conformation but agility and alertness. And a great deal's at stake at these events. Anyway, I whistled then yelled at Herbie, the horse in front, to pick up the pace, but the owner would have none of it. We had harsh words, and it got out of hand. Wexford panicked and charged through the crowd. You prevented more casualties."

I decided not to mention that I was a guest of Ross McConnell, the man he'd provoked.

As we neared the parking area, Wexford's owner removed his cap and smoothed back his unruly hair. "I understand you're acquainted with Wexford's half brother?"

"I'm not sure. Who would that be?" I asked.

"Your friend."

"Sorry?"

"Clancy!"

I stopped in my tracks and laughed. "Clancy's Wexford's half brother? I can't believe it!"

I stroked Wexford's silky jaw. "Well, they're both handsome, big guys "

"Miss Porter, would you like to hunt with us tomorrow – with the Blazers?"

"I don't have a horse," I replied.

He laughed and patted my shoulder. "You could ride Clancy himself. You wouldn't even have to leave home – the meet's at St. Cleran's – 9:00 a.m."

"Are you serious? I thought he was reserved by Lady so-and-so?"

"I'm employed by Lady Biddle-Jones. Do all her lorry work, mainly moving Clancy to and from meets. She had a conflict in London and has left me in charge. Do you have riding clothes?"

I nodded. "Just my boots and cap, but I understand the hotel can fill in."

"Perfect! And you can be my guest at the hunt breakfast afterwards. We'd have a merry time! Are you on board then?"

I adjusted my cap, trying to decide. Since this man had exchanged fighting words with McConnell, should I first check with Ross? Oh, what the heck. "All right. Count me in. With Clancy, I think I'm up to it!"

He grabbed my hand and shook it. "Excellent! 'Tis settled then....Now come along while I load Wexford."

He rested his massive arm on my shoulder as he led Wexford toward his trailer and explained where the Blazers would rendezvous in the morning. There was a gentle strength about this man that assured me I'd be safe with him, whether tearing cross-country or chasing bad guys.

I suddenly stopped. "Wait....I don't know your name."

He pointed toward the shiny, eight-horse trailer just ahead – GRADY QUINN HORSE TRANSPORT. Oh no! This was the man who'd worked for Sean O'Malley – the same man who'd picked up the stolen horses from Jimmy Craigh.

15

By the time I returned to the conformation arena, a different show was underway. I looked around for McConnell. Nowhere in sight. And Herbie wasn't in the ring. Then I spotted them on the far side of the grounds, Ross holding Herbie's lead and engaged in an intense conversation with a group of men. I suspected it might be about selling the horse. Ross waved, handed Herbie to one of his associates and strolled in my direction.

"Hi! I didn't think you'd made it. Did you see the show?" he asked.

This was not the time or place to explain that I'd missed it because I'd been racing cross-country after Wexford. "Sorry, I arrived late. Did Herbie ribbon?"

"He won a fourth – which wasn't bad, considering what happened. I'll explain later." Glancing back at the men, he added, "P.J., I have some information to share with you, but not here. There's a pub up the road where we could talk."

I was suspicious of his motive. I liked Ross all right, but with Simon still on my mind, I felt it was unfair to encourage him. Also, I believed that given the opportunity, Ross could become a pest.

When I hesitated, he added more urgently, "If you have plans, we won't stay long. *The Troubles* is just three miles up the road toward your hotel. You could drive ahead – I'd be there promptly. You'll be interested in what I have to report."

"*The Troubles*....sounds dreary," I said.

"Dreary from the outside, but don't be fooled. 'Tis lively and full of history."

"Ross, I'm sorry. I need to get back and make some phone calls to the states. Can't you tell me now?"

He touched my shoulder. "Please. Tell Dempsey, the owner, to park you in a quiet booth."

Feeling guilty about accepting a riding invitation from Grady Quinn without consulting Ross, I suppose I owed him. "All right, but don't be long."

Then, recalling how difficult it was to locate anything in rural Ireland, I added, "You promise it's easy to find?"

"Ah. Just off the road on the right – looks like a rock barn with the windows boarded up. There's a sign in front. Check three miles on your odometer from the center of Kilcolgan. You'll be all right."

"If I'm not there, call out the gardai!"

He chuckled and hustled back to his associates.

At 2.9 miles, I spotted a field full of cars and trucks,

including trailers with horses peering out of their Dutch doors. Then I saw the sign, small and almost unreadable. I pulled in and parked as close as possible to the entrance.

At one time, the two story building might have been used as a barn, but now the windows and hay doors were sealed.

I found the entrance on one side of the building. Inside, I was rocked back on my heels with an explosion of loud music, high spirits and crammed humanity. I squeezed into the congested room. The crowd seemed to be pushing in a clockwise direction, so I fell into the flow. From their clothes, I'd guess they were mostly locals who'd stopped in after the draft show. There was also a handful of foxhunters in elegant stock ties and English boots, and a few out-of-place tourists.

The room was made of weathered brick with an oak beam and rafter ceiling. A mahogany bar ran the length of the far wall. Above it was a blemished mirror that measured maybe ten feet by six. Across the glass was scrolled in white paint – YOUR TROUBLES ARE OVER – HAVE A DRINK!

This place was much too noisy for a meeting with Ross. But as I turned to leave, an unshaven man with a gray pony tail, and balancing a tray of food, called, "Miss Porter! Miss Porter! Hold on!"

He worked his way toward me but his progress was slowed by customers reaching to grab whatever he was carrying. As he came closer, I recognized what it was – *boiled pigs' feet*. He must be offering them for free, I thought. Who'd pay good money for anything so grotesque?

He shouted, "If you're McConnell's friend, he called to say you were coming!"

"How'd you recognize me?"

He laughed. "I can spot an American a mile away. Follow me, miss."

Lifting his platter high, he called out, "Coming through! Coming through!"

A muscular customer with his sleeves rolled up and his tweed cap turned sideways, yelled to me. "Would you have a drink with me, miss?" I was momentarily tempted but ignored him and bulldozed on.

I was pleased to discover that the dim adjoining room, lined with dark oak booths and decorated with antique firearms and tarnished lanterns, was nearly empty. A familiar Irish ballad was being piped in. Most of *The Troubles*' patrons obviously preferred the high-density action in the barroom.

The tray-toting waiter pointed toward a bench where I could observe the other customers. "I'm Walter Dempsey," he said. "They call me Jack – like your fighter. Shall I have one of the girls bring you a Guinness?"

"Thank you. I'd like that."

A deep scar on Dempsey's temple was partially covered by his long hair. The disfigurement was difficult to ignore and reminded me of a war wound.

He lowered his tray. "Back there, I saw you frowning at the house specialty. Please now, try one."

"I don't believe I care for any, but thanks."

He shook his head. "Ah, you haven't been in a real Irish pub 'til you've sampled pigs' feet with black beer." He tilted the tray so that I could have a better look. "Just one bite – sprinkle it with sea salt. Go on, now."

I studied the selection – pink, puckered and repulsive.

"You won't be invited back," he warned with a crooked grin. I assumed he had nerve damage at the corner of his mouth, maybe connected to his head wound. How had that happened, I wondered?

Removing my ball cap and gritting my teeth, I said, "All right! I'll sample one."

"Lay out this napkin," he said, handing me a sheet of ordinary brown paper. With a pair of tongs, he set a huge pig's foot in front of me. "If it's easier, this first time, hold your nose." He laughed and hustled off to serve his boisterous clientele.

From here I could see into the barroom where Dempsey's customers were nibbling on the house special with one hand while quaffing beer with the other. That gave me courage. I waited several minutes for my Guinness to arrive and for my resolve to take hold. Finally, I grabbed the pink meat by the hoof, added a smidgen of salt, took a swig of beer, raised the foot to my mouth, closed my eyes, clasped my nose and chomped down.

As I waited for my palate to react, someone with a masculine voice asked, "How is it? There, there, no need to turn green. Delicious, right?"

I hesitated and tried to smile. "Not half bad!"

I glanced up. "Mr. Quinn, I wasn't expecting you!"

16

Quinn sat down opposite me in the booth. With his cap off, his rumpled hair fell to his collar. Broad forehead, flat nose and unflinching eyes suggested he might have been in a fight or two – maybe professionally. At the same time, he moved with the bearing of a gentleman – a regular country squire, I thought.

Still, a hidden flaw might motivate him to steal horses. At the Oklahoma Police Academy, I'd learned there are nuts who'd steal anything just for the thrill. "Don't judge a horse by its teeth, alone," my father used to say.

"Please, call me Grady," he said, resting his Guinness on a soiled coaster. "Are you expecting someone?"

I shifted in my seat and pushed back my hair. "I'm meeting Sergeant Ross McConnell."

"Uh oh!" he said, leaning back in the bench. "I'm glad you told me." He took a sip of beer. "No matter, himself may be a while. Tom Lynch wants to buy his horse, Herbie, but Tom'll try to wear him down, first."

I was still concerned what might happen if Ross showed up while Grady was with me. But I couldn't control that. If a confrontation ensued, I'd exit left. It wasn't my war.

"How do you know McConnell?" Quinn asked.

When I'd caught Wexford, Quinn had mentioned that he'd heard about me. He probably knew more than he let on, including my meeting with Ross. But since it was Quinn who'd transported the stolen horses from Jimmy Craigh's farm to Shannon Airport, I thought I should be open and friendly. Maybe he'd share a tip that would lead me to the cache.

I explained how, as a favor to U.S. friends, I'd stopped in Galway City to check on O'Malley. I'd met Sergeant McConnell at police headquarters while making inquiries. He informed me that O'Malley had committed suicide. I didn't share with him that I'd just learned O'Malley was actually alive, and that an unidentified body had been spotted at the Cliffs.

"Sean O'Malley was a friend of mine," he said. "And I transported many a horse for him. When I heard he'd switched those horses, I couldn't believe it. He didn't seem the type."

Though time was short and this the wrong setting in which to ask questions, I couldn't resist one. "Grady, what do you think O'Malley did with those horses?"

He swept back a fist full of hair and furrowed his brow. "Ah, similar thefts have been perpetrated before in

Ireland, but the animals were never found. It was rumored they may have ended up in Europe – to be used as breeding stock or shown under new names with forged passports. But, to this day, the thieves remain unknown."

He paused and leaned forward. "Pardon me – I've nothing against Americans, but I've thought all along the purchasers in the U.S. should be investigated. Insurance fraud, you know. And what about the buyer's transport agent in America? Did they check him out? There are number of possibilities other than O'Malley."

I nodded. Right then, I decided to telephone Simon as soon as I returned to St. Clerans. It was time for him to become involved from the U.S. end.

I glanced around the dining room. It was somber and in need of some freshening up. Maybe an off-white ceiling, retaining the dark beams, with bright hunt posters on the walls would liven things up. But it occurred to me that the bleakness went with the name of the place.

"Grady, *The Troubles* is an unusual name, even for a pub," I said. "Where did that come from?"

"For sure, it's an odd name for a place of good cheer. Dempsey, the owner, came up with that. Most people here don't care for it. The name refers to the painful history of Ireland."

I searched his eyes. "Tell me about that, Grady, if you don't mind."

"Well, Dempsey is not from around here – he's from Belfast – Northern Ireland called Ulster. In the late 1960s, he fought in the IRA against the occupying British forces. Story is he used this place as an armory for hiding illegal arms, smuggled in from Boston. Other than that, Dempsey's life is pretty much a mystery, except his face confirms the rumor that he took a grenade during a skirmish with the English and almost died in a Galway hospital. But he won't talk about it. Who knows – the British could still be searching for him."

"He's probably a hero around here," I said.

Grady nodded and turned away.

I surveyed the crowd in the barroom to make sure McConnell hadn't arrived. Not in sight, but he could be buried among the packed revelers, trying to buy a beer.

"But why *The Troubles*?" I pressed. I was curious about this bit of Irish history. I thought of Simon who was a trivia buff. He would've been intrigued.

"Most of the current generation believe *The Troubles* refers to the conflict between Catholics and Protestants in Ulster, beginning with the marches and rioting of 1968.

"The old folks and others, like myself, still hold The Troubles came with Oliver Cromwell and the British in the 1650s. His army butchered the Irish and confiscated their lands, particularly in the north, to be resettled by English and Scottish Protestants.

"And when the Great Irish Famine started in 1845 and millions starved, the English turned their back on us."

Quinn shook his head and his eyes moistened. "'Tis all painful, ancient history," he added. "Since the Belfast

Agreement of 1998, which restored power-sharing self-government in Ulster, life has improved. But in my opinion, 'tis a hangover that even Irish whiskey will never cure."

He bowed his head. "I'm content with life here. I'll never leave. But there are men who fought the English in the IRA, like Dempsey, who'll take their hatred to the grave."

Quinn seemed deeply moved by his own words and rubbed an eye. "P.J., that's all I have to say about that – and if you don't mind, I'll bid you goodnight." To my surprise, he slid out of the booth. "See you around eight in the morning, on the road just outside St. Clerans. I'll have Clancy saddled. Better wear a rain jacket – weather report is damp."

I did my best to smile. "I'll be there, Grady."

What a sensitive, bear of a man, I thought.

With his head down, he disappeared into the merry makers, who were exuberantly singing:

When Irish eyes are smiling, sure it's
like a morning Spring
    In the lilt of Irish laughter, you can
hear the angels sing.

Not exactly Quinn's version of conditions in this country. But the problems of Ireland were not mine. Still, I sympathized with the years of misery they must have endured. I couldn't help but compare their plight with that of my Cherokee ancestors.

17

By the time McConnell arrived, a bearded patron had climbed on the bar and, with arms flailing, was directing the singing.

> *When Irish hearts are happy,*
> *all the world seems bright and gay*
> *And when Irish eyes are*
> *smiling, sure they steal your heart*
> *away.*

The lyrics were haunting. Unexplainably, I thought of Simon – was he capable of such misty-eyed sentiment?

Ross tossed his plaid cap on the table, and I snapped back to reality. "Sorry I'm late," he said.

Out of uniform, the dashing Sergeant McConnell could also pass for landed gentry – Wellington boots, corduroy pants and Harris tweed jacket with suede elbows.

"Did you sell Herbie?" I asked.

"No, I tried to, but no one would meet my price."

The waitress brought McConnell a Guinness. I declined another – wasn't quite finished with my first. The Irish glass of dark beer contained twenty ounces – equivalent to a bottle and half of our brew.

"Ross, if you don't mind, how much were you asking for him?"

"Ah, I would have taken 50,000 euros, about $75,000, but we couldn't strike a bargain."

My jaw dropped. "$75,000! Isn't that a lot for Herbie?"

Ross shook his head. "Not atall. He could have earned that in stud fees in two to three years."

"No wonder swindlers want to steal Irish horses."

McConnell quaffed the foam off his beer. "P.J., that's why I wanted to talk to you. During the show, I received a call from Warden Paddy Nolan at the Cliffs of Moher. His team recovered that body you spotted."

I knew it couldn't be O'Malley, but I didn't want to let on. "Was it O'Malley?" I asked.

"No, it wasn't. Now we suspect O'Malley may have murdered this person and dumped the body in the ocean. Remember we found O'Malley's truck and cap at the cliffs."

"Do you know who the dead person is?"

Ross lowered his head. "I suppose it will be common knowledge by tomorrow. He's been identified as the Government Equine Inspector at Shannon Airport – Doyle Crouch."

How curious. Jimmy Craigh had mentioned Inspector Crouch. He had processed the stolen horses for shipment to Kennedy International.

"Evidence of foul play?" I asked.

"The body was mutilated and bloated almost beyond recognition. But the coroner will take a closer look."

I nodded. "You indicated O'Malley might be responsible for Crouch's death. Other than the truck and cap, do you have any proof?"

"None yet," Ross replied, shaking his head. "But where is he? If O'Malley's innocent of stealing those horses and not involved in Crouch's death, why doesn't he come forward? Bring his solicitor, if he wants."

I wasn't satisfied. "Could there be a connection between O'Malley and Crouch?"

"Well, O'Malley himself was in the business of selling horses, and Crouch was responsible for shipping them abroad. We'll be investigating that association once we receive the Coroner's report."

Ross and I sat back and sipped our beers as the customers sang:

For the spring-time of life is the sweetest of all
There is ne'er a real care or regret
And while spring-time is ours, throughout all of youth's hours
Let us smile each chance we get

Finally, I reached across the table and touched his hand. "Ross, thank you for informing me about the body. You didn't have to share that. Now, I need to get back to St. Clerans and report this to the Devereuxs. They'll want to know O'Malley's probably alive."

He nodded. "I understand. If I learn more, P.J., I'll be letting you know."

I slid to the edge of the booth.

Ross raised his hand. "Before you leave, there's something else I'd like to mention."

"Sure, what is it?" I asked.

"I'll be hunting tomorrow with the Blazers at St. Clerans. Would you like to join us? You could ride Herbie – he'd take good care of ye."

Oh my! This was embarrassing. "Ross, I'm sorry. I've already made plans to hunt in the morning. I'm riding Clancy."

"Really. Who might you be riding with?"

I stood to leave, slipping on my cap. "Grady Quinn," I announced.

He sprang to his feet, face inflamed, one arm waving. "What! Not Quinn! P.J., you couldn't!"

"I'm sorry." But having no adequate answer, I gave him a quick hug and dashed for the door.

When Irish eyes are smiling, sure they steal your heart away

As I searched for my car in the congested lot, I passed Herbie, head and neck hanging out his trailer window, searching for his master. I patted his nose. "Good boy! Sorry I'm riding Clancy tomorrow! Another time, maybe!"

18

Back in my room at St. Clerans, I made arrangements for additional riding gear for tomorrow's hunt, including a rain jacket. Then I devoured a generous bowl of lamb stew and French bread slathered with butter, climbed into my luxurious, oversized bed and telephoned Simon.

"It's P.J. What're you doing? How's law school?" I asked.

"Hi! I'm having lunch – all alone. And I'm in the middle of orientation – classes start in two days." He paused. "Glad you called. I've got some news for you."

I punched up my pillow. "I have a lot to tell you, too. You first."

Simon hesitated as if to collect his thoughts. "I've been doing some research, mostly on the Internet. Have you heard that in the last eighteen months there were two other horse thefts – same scenario – big-time show jumpers switched between Ireland and New York?"

"Both the breeder and the transport agent over here

mentioned that, but I haven't learned the particulars," I replied.

"Two horses were shipped to Houston and another to Philadelphia. All three were counterfeits. The buyer from Philly settled for the insurance money. The family from Houston offered fifty thousand dollars for the recovery of their two. If we can get to the bottom of this, we're in line for a possible quarter million. Can you imagine?"

"That's a lot of money," I said, mentally clicking off a few luxuries I would indulge in. "Maybe if we locate the horses O'Malley shipped, we'll find the others, too. But, before we get carried away, let me update you on what's happened over here."

"I'm all ears."

I reported that O'Malley was not dead but in hiding, that I'd talked to him and he wanted my help. To complicate his case, the body of a drowned man, thought to be O'Malley, was recovered and identified as Doyle Crouch, a government shipping official – the same person who processed the stolen horses that were airlifted to the U.S. Because of minor evidence at the scene, the police now suspect that O'Malley murdered Crouch.

"Have you reported this to Kit?" he asked.

"Not yet. I planned to do that right after we hang up. Have you talked to her recently?" I asked.

"I did – last night. She hopes you'll stay over there 'til O'Malley's case is resolved. Expense is no problem. I explained to her that we were also trying to find the stolen horses to earn the reward money. She said, 'Go for it! It might help O'Malley's case.'"

"Good. That's a green light, then," I said, pleased that the Devereuxs had such deep pockets.

"What's our next move, P.J.? Any ideas?"

I popped in one of the pillow-top chocolates and pulled the luxuriant down comforter to my neck. "I haven't a clue who stole those horses, but I don't believe it was O'Malley," I said. "He doesn't strike me as the criminal type. As for the other players, I'm not certain.

"Since we have nothing to go on, yet, we need to study the small stuff. Remember what Detective Stan Tobin preached in Oklahoma City when we solved the *Mink and Manure Murders* – 'if in doubt, start at both ends and work toward the middle.' Simon, you should talk to the Farrells and the vet that examined the phony horses in Texas. Also, if you can manage it, check out the transport records at Kennedy International."

"I'll see what I can uncover here," P.J. added. "And we should both make inquiries about forged passports and how microchip switching could be done."

"There's another angle to consider," Simon said.

"What's that?"

"After Kennedy, the horses went to the New York Animal Import Center, a secured federal facility up the Hudson. They would have stayed there at least three days for infectious disease tests. What do we do about that? Going through government channels to access their records would take forever. Could your sergeant friend help?"

"He's not a friend, but McConnell might have connections," I said with an edge.

Of course Ross McConnell was a friend. Why bother to deny it?

I tried to sound indifferent. "I expect to see him tomorrow, and I'll ask. I'm going foxhunting with the Galway Blazers, and everyone in the county is supposed to be there – over two hundred riders. Might be a good opportunity to ask questions."

"You're hunting with the Blazers! How'd you swing that? They're supposed to be so exclusive – members only!"

Simon sounded jealous! Good!

I was tempted to disclose that two men, who both seemed interested in me, had invited me to hunt. And to add to the drama, they'd both be riding. Though that might provoke more jealously in Simon, which would be fun, it would only sidetrack our effort, so I skipped it.

"The hotel owns horses, and I've been provided a big Irish Draft by the name of Clancy. He's fabulous! I'm excited but a bit nervous. Do you have any advice for a relative novice?" I asked.

"Mm....I do have a couple suggestions....keep in mind these are second hand."

"Let's hear them," I said, sitting up.

"There'll be lots of flask passing, and that stuff's potent – so go easy. Also, you'll probably be jumping forty to fifty walls during the course of the day and leaping off twenty or so banks with big drops. My advice is – keep your heels low, legs forward and never look down!"

"What! Why never look down?"

"The Irish don't bother much with the grooming of landing areas, so your horse will probably be dodging loose rocks and debris. Scary for the rider, but the horses are used to it."

"Now I'm worried."

Simon laughed. "You'll do fine. Just trust Clancy. Still, I'll say a prayer for you, just in case."

"Thanks, I may need it," I joked.

"P.J., back to the reward money, I have an idea I'd like to run by you."

"What's that?" I asked. The tone of his voice made me uneasy.

"If I'm in law school, I won't have time to talk to the Farrells in Dallas and do the other running around. I ought to talk to Georgetown, see if I can transfer to the January term and re-start with you."

"Simon, that's the best idea you've ever had! Give it a try! But don't forget our agreement."

"Refresh my memory," he said, chuckling.

"If that ever happened, we pledged to share books, notes, maybe a dorm suite – but not a bed."

"Ha! How could I forget? We may have to discuss that further," Simon quipped.

I chuckled. "Good night, partner."

19

A continental breakfast was delivered to the room at seven. I opened the curtains. It was raining and gloomy. I picked up the phone and rang the front desk. "I'm supposed to hunt with the Blazers today. Will they be going out in this weather?"

"Ah, makes no difference to the Blazers, miss. They'll hunt, rain or shine."

"A hardy group!"

"That they are. Even when it snows, they ride, miss."

"Thank you." This would make the footing slippery and jumping even more dangerous. But I couldn't renege without meeting with Grady. He would have gotten an early start to collect and saddle the horses, and would be waiting for me. If I only had his cell phone.

I zipped up my jacket, adjusted the collar and plunged into the chilly rain. Not knowing exactly where Grady was parked, I started down the main road, hopping over the larger puddles, heel-walking through the rest.

The weather hadn't dampened the spirits of man nor beast. Of the estimated two hundred plus participants, no one was complaining or threatening to throw in their rain-soaked towel and go home. On the contrary, hearty greetings and repartee rang through the mist.

The confusion of so many vehicles, horses and riders made it difficult to rendezvous with companions. Five minutes from the hotel, I spotted Grady and Clancy, drenched to the skin, waiting on the shoulder of the road. Recognizing I was miffed with the weather, he greeted me with a broad smile and an encouraging pat on the shoulder. "I'm glad you didn't change your mind. 'Tis just a gentle Irish mist."

"Are you kidding? It's pouring!" I declared.

I tried to appear positive. "I'd be lying if I said I didn't consider going back to bed."

"Right, I'm pleased you didn't," he said, grinning. "Besides, those big dark eyes are beautiful in the rain. A pleasure to behold."

I chuckled. "Is that a bit of Irish blarney? If it is, I don't mind at all – I mean *atall*."

"Not *atall*," he joked. "'Tis a fact."

Grady's jacket accentuated his powerful upper body. He easily weighed two hundred and twenty-five pounds and needed a husky horse like Wexford to carry him. Was it possible this authentic outdoorsman and horse lover could also be a criminal?

I peered into Clancy's doleful eyes and rubbed his

soft, damp nose. Droplets of rain trickled down his face and dripped from his chin. He acknowledged me with a bewildered look but nuzzled my hand and nickered a friendly greeting. He appeared confused over being asked to jump around the countryside in these conditions, but if I insisted, he seemed willing.

Olive-colored, waxed-cotton coats and jackets were the order of the day. But the Master and his staff remained formal in scarlet frock coats made of dense melton. Though water repellant, if the rain continued, they'd become soaked and surely have to be exchanged.

Grady tightened my collar. "It can't stay like this," he cooed. "The hunting gods and luck of the Irish won't allow it."

"Have you heard the weather report?"

He shook the water off his cap and laughed. "We don't rely on meteorology like you Americans. We just go and trust in the Lord."

I kicked at the soggy turf. "Fine, but isn't the footing dangerous?"

"Not atall!" he joked. "The horses are used to it, so we pretend to ignore it."

"Maybe I could see better, if I had steeplechase goggles."

Grady shook his head. "Those are for flying mud. In the rain, they would only make the visibility worse. Just lower your head – your helmet will help cut through."

As the time to mount approached, riders and horses

milled about, trying to hook up with friends. I looked around for Ross McConnell – nowhere in sight. But, through the drizzle, I did spot a vaguely familiar woman in a smart rain jacket, pulling a flashy white mare. Then it registered – it was Fiona McBride, Ross's friend, the waitress from the hotel. Despite her horse's resistance, she seemed undaunted by the conditions, exchanging greetings with other riders, mainly young men.

A tall rider in a felt top hat, dripping buckets, cantered by. "Top of the morn'in to ya, Grady!" he called.

He tipped his hat to me. "Patience, miss! 'Tis going to be a lovely day!"

I mustered a broad smile with a salute. How can these people be drenched and chilled and still so upbeat? But I had to admit, their high spirits were contagious.

When the Huntsman sounded *Moving Out*, Grady gave me a leg up. Clancy turned and nosed my boot as if to say, *Not to worry – I'll take care of you*. Tall order considering the downpour, but still, I was somehow warmed by the anticipation of riding him.

Once Grady was saddled, he reached into his coat pocket and pulled out a silver flask.

"What've you got there?" I asked, knowing full well.

"'Tis port with a little umph added. Perfect to jump start this dismal day."

I laughed. Just the thought of it lightened my mood.

He took a long swig and passed it to me. "Never too early for a bit of Dutch courage when hunting!"

"Oh, why not! Here's looking at you!" I took a sip… then another. It was delicious and sent a bolt of warmth and bravery through my body. "That hit the spot! I can't see much in this rain, but whatever's coming, bring it on!"

Toward the end of the road, the riders maneuvered into columns four or five horses wide, moving toward the excited cries of the hounds. Eighteen couples were out on this special occasion.

"How are these hounds going to hunt in this downpour?" I asked. "Seems impossible for scenting."

"'Twill be a hunt-by-sight day. Not to worry, Master knows where to stir up some sport."

Within moments, we were out of sight of St. Clerans, leaving behind the lorries and trailer trucks, parked along the road and in adjoining fields. Grady and I rode in the center of the long column. Because of the poor visibility, all the riders looked alike. But one gentlemen's helmeted head bobbed above the others. It was Ross McConnell on Herbie. And by his side was Fiona, laughing at some intimate joke.

During my dinner with Ross, I suspected there'd been a romantic connection between them that had gone *caput,* but now, they seemed to have repaired their relationship.

Grady nudged my arm and pointed. "There's a large covert about two hundred yards from here. 'Tis full of fox. The hounds will be cast there, and we'll be off at a gallop. You'll see. I know these walls and banks, so stay on my tail. Clancy's courageous. He won't refuse. Just sit up and hold on…and try to smile, will you, please?"

We both laughed. "I'll try," I said. Easy for him to say.

Clancy looked around as if to confirm that I was ready. I patted him on the shoulder "I'm so lucky to be out with a grand guy like you, Clancy." I said. "I wish someone would take a picture of us."

Grady squeezed my shoulder. "Should we face a ditch, some of the Field will take it on. You and I won't. The edges will be soft and treacherous, so I'll lead you around. 'Tis not a good day for swimming! Are you with me?"

"Gotcha!" I replied. As enthusiastic as I'd been, we must be insane riding in this weather, I thought. We couldn't see twenty yards ahead. But Clancy's placid temperament, along with the port, gave me unexpected confidence. "Grady, I'll follow you anywhere – within reason, of course."

"Right – I like your style." He reached over and squeezed my hand. Grady was a man's man with a touch of gentleness which most women, myself included, were drawn to.

Somewhere in the mist, the hounds began to bay. The Huntsman blew *Gone Away*, and the horses pranced to the mounting tension.

As though it were scripted, the rain diminished to a soupy mist, and the clouds lightened to gray. Our pace quickened to a fast trot – Clancy preferred a collected canter, about the same speed, which was also my favorite. He clopped and sloshed though the mud with a dancer's rhythm. We were *simpatico*. Grady motioned across the meadow. "The fox will try to escape by running in a mile-wide circle. He'll take us over one wall after another. If the hounds get too close, *Charlie* will throw in a couple of ditches to lose us. If Clancy falls behind, don't spur him, just a squeeze with your leg will do."

"I've got it, *mein fuhrer*."

Grady scowled, then laughed and pinched my arm.

The screams and howls of the hounds grew louder. The Huntsman gave another blast on his horn, and the stride accelerated to a gallop. The Field spread out to avoid collisions. Before I could focus on how to negotiate the obstacles that lay ahead, Clancy had carried me over a four foot wall and turned toward another.

"Good boy, Clancy!" I blurted, grasping his mane. He jumped that so easily – like Transport over a two foot log.

Clearing the second wall, I could barely see that the horses in front were jumping a third, then making a ninety degree turn to the right on a blacktop road. The last time I made a sharp turn on wet asphalt, the horse slid out from under me, and I broke my leg and ruined a perfectly good saddle.

But this time was different. Clancy took the wall, slowed, then turned sharply on the slick pavement like a skier executing a turn on the side of a mountain – body nearly erect with his weight on the outside. Who'd taught him the principles of downhill racing, I wondered?

When the road angled to the left, we flew straight ahead, over more stone walls. The obstacles were coming so often that I finally relaxed and let Clancy run the show. The sloppy footing didn't seem to bother him, and we developed a synchronized jumping ballet with Grady and Wexford. If the visibility were better, it would have even been fun.

Grady turned and yelled, "Ditch ahead! Stay with me!" He pulled his horse to the left though most of the Field kicked on, committed to leaping the ten-foot wide ravine. I kept one eye on Grady and the other on the courageous thrusters.

Through the mist, I spotted Fiona McBride as she booted and yelled, "Come on Maddy! Let's go!"

Ross was galloping on her flank. Twenty yards from the edge, he appeared to flag down Fiona, jerked his horse away from the ditch and skidded to a halt. Fiona's mount was startled and jumped off balance and crashed into the far embankment with its forelegs clawing at the rim. It twisted, fell backwards and disappeared into the gorge.

I nearly screamed out, in fear for Fiona. I wanted to stop and check on her, but protocol demanded I stay with Grady and the Field. It seemed a heartless rule, but it was my understanding that accidents were to be attended by riding companions or staff.

Before I could alert Grady, he was skidding his way down a shallow section of the ditch, and I was obliged to follow, concentrating on my balance and gripping Clancy's mane.

Wexford scrambled to the top of the other side then sprung forward, set on catching the Field.

Reaching the high ground, I urged Clancy into a gallop. Closing the gap, I called, "Grady! – Grady! Fiona McBride fell in the ravine back there!"

He pulled up. "Who? Oh! Did anyone stop to help?"

I shook my head, water spraying off my cap. "I don't know! I was set on following you!"

He looked back, but the haze was too thick to see much. "Wait right here! Don't leave! The Field Master needs to know! Anyone falling in that mud and water today will have a rough time climbing out!" He turned Wexford toward the disappearing Field and galloped off, leaving me to wonder if Ross had tried to help.

As I stoked Clancy's neck, he stood quietly, despite his natural instinct to race after the stragglers galloping by. No Thoroughbred would be so patient. But he used the opportunity to violently shimmy the water off his dripping body, nearly shedding me in the process.

Grady had been gone a few moments when, out of the mist, rode Ross McConnell. He spotted me and stopped, nervously looking around. "Which way'd the Field go?" he asked.

"Straight ahead. What about Fiona?"

He shook his head. "Haven't seen her!" Then he spurred his horse in the direction of the others.

How could that be? I was almost certain they were riding together, and that it was Fiona who'd plunged into the ravine. Why had he lied to me? Something was wrong. I wished Grady hadn't left me.

In the distance, I could hear the Huntsman sounding *Going Home*. Moments later, Grady, hidden in the fog, called out. "P.J., can you hear me? Where are you?"

"Over here!" I yelled. "Over here!"

He followed the sound of my voice and soon halted alongside.

"The hunt's been cancelled," he said. "Come on – we're going back to St. Clerans. Visibility ahead is deteriorating and footing has become dangerous. Several horses have fallen, and somebody's been fished out of a drainage ditch."

"Ha! I could've told the Master that conditions were too tricky before we started."

"Now, now, be a good sport. Let's head in," he said, offering me a drink from his flask which I greedily took.

"I hope Fiona's all right. I had the oddest encounter with Ross McConnell."

"What happened?" he asked, slipping the miniature jug back into his coat pocket.

"Let's go in and dry off." I turned Clancy for home. I reviewed what I thought I'd seen, just before her fall. Halting at the brink of the ditch, Ross had signaled Fiona to stop. Now I believed it was not that but a snap of his whip intended to spook her horse.

20

The hunt breakfast was a buffet in the St. Clerans' lounge – a spacious, paneled room, with beamed ceilings and threadbare Persian rugs. The furniture, mostly leather, had been moved to the perimeter to accommodate the gathering. On one side of the room, a panoramic bay window overlooked the meadow where Clancy usually grazed.

By the time we'd unsaddled and blanketed the horses, disposed of our rain gear and spruced up, there was standing room only. Grady grabbed a couple of beers from a circulating waiter. He extended his glass and met mine with a clink. "May the morn break with the warmth of the sun and friendships intact," he said with a wink.

"I'll drink to that."

He studied me up and down and said in his thick brogue, "P.J., I'm impressed. You're a good sport. Even Lady Biddle-Jones, a true thruster, wouldn't have ridden today. Have you considered emigrating to the Emerald Isle? You have the spirit and fairness of a bonnie Irish lass."

"Thank you, sir. I hadn't considered relocating. But as long as compliments are flying, I have one for you."

Grady leaned back. "Now be careful, lass!"

"From the start of the hunt, I realized you were an expert horseman and would lead me and Clancy around safely. So, despite the treacherous footing, I sort of relaxed and had a good time today, or at least, a memorable one."

He touched my arm. "'Tis generous of you. I'm pleased you feel that way."

So Grady Quinn was a bull of a man with a tender side.

While we were sweet-talking, I'd been aware that instead of the raucous, St. Paddy's celebration I'd expected, something was dampening the spirit of the occasion. I guessed it was the dismal weather, along with the hunt being cut short.

"Doesn't the crowd seem a bit subdued?" I asked. "Thought there'd be toasts – maybe some singing."

"You're right. This is not a good omen," Grady said with a frown.

"What's wrong?"

He looked around. "In the formative years, the Blazers experienced a *blank* hunting day, no prey to chase, similar to this morning. The breakfast afterwards was at a popular pub named the Crock of Gold. The mood was glum. After several Guinnesses, one malcontent tried to liven the party by starting a fire on the bar. Unfortunately, it got out of control and burnt the Crock to the ground. Hence the name – Galway Blazers."

"Are you kidding?" Sounded like an American fish story.

"Not atall. I wasn't around then so I won't swear to it," he said with a sly grin. "But most believe it to be true."

Before I could challenge that story, there was a tinkling of glasses and a hush fell over the gathering. A staff member in a scarlet frock coat stood on a chair and raised his arm for silence. "I'm Joint Master Padraig Ryan. 'Tis a sad day in the history of the Blazers. Some of you may not have heard – one of our regulars, attempting to jump a ditch, fell beneath her mount and drowned. Though many of you already know who it was, I've been asked not to release the name until relatives have been informed."

He paused and looked around the room. "All are saddened, I know, but Blazer tradition holds we offer a toast to the passing member and carry on. Now please join me. Raise your glasses to bid farewell to our fallen companion."

Lifting his glass, the Joint Master turned, gesturing to the members. "Valiant departed friend and member, may you continue to celebrate the hunt for eternity with the generations of departed Blazers on those lush green pastures in the hereafter. And may God ride with you, good and faithful comrade!"

"Here! Here!" the group exclaimed.

No one had a way with words like the Irish, I thought. This was followed by whispers and hushed discussion, everyone attempting to confirm the name of the deceased. Of course, Grady and I knew. It was Fiona Bride.

I sensed Grady tightening up and looking around. "Wait here," he said, then muscled his way through the crowd. He was headed toward Ross McConnell who towered a foot above the others.

A heated conversation between them quickly escalated into a shouting match. Fearing the worst, I pushed through the throng. Grady was yelling, "Don't lie to me, McConnell! You were there! Why didn't you take care of her?"

"You're wrong! I don't know what you're talking about!" Ross roared back.

The crowd backed away. A brawl at this moment would not only disrupt this solemn occasion but could damage property for which Grady and I might be held responsible.

In a flash, Ross clenched his fist and swung. Grady jerked back, but the blow grazed his head and staggered him.

This quarrel was my fault. I never should have told Grady what I thought I'd seen in the mist. I could have been mistaken. Too late now. Ross was strong, but no match for this powerful man. I considered jumping between them but concluded that could be fatal – to me.

As Grady was about to fire back with a crushing blow, I resorted to my police training and rushed him, ramming my shoulder into his chest. He was caught off guard, and the two of us went flying onto a nearby settee, me landing hard on top. Momentarily stunned, we lay there, ignoring a circle of shocked spectators.

Grady's fierce expression relaxed. "P.J., what in the world are you doing?" His expression slowly mutated into a broad smile – then he began to chuckle. "P.J., this is neither the time nor place for fooling around!"

"No fighting, please!" I demanded with a grin.

While the audience stared wide-eyed, we began to laugh, softly at first, then uncontrollably. It took several long moments to compose ourselves. Embarrassed, we scrambled to our feet and looked around. Ross was nowhere in sight. He'd missed all the fun.

I thought we should apologize to the Master, but Grady whispered into my hair, "Let's get out of here." Grabbing my hand, he pulled me through the crowd toward the door.

Once Grady'd collected his rain gear, we lingered in the hotel lobby. "Despite everything, it's been unforgettable. Thank you," I said. "Sorry for the body slam. Do you need any help with the horses?"

He smiled. "Right, no damage done. And I'll take care of Clancy and Wexford – no trouble atall."

"Give Clancy a hug for me. He was amazing. I had no idea there were such horses."

"I'll do that. The feeling is obviously mutual. P.J., can we get together again, maybe tomorrow?"

I hesitated while several thoughts raced through my

mind.

I'd developed a trust, possibly more, for Grady Quinn, even though there was still a possibility he could be involved in the crime.

My intuition told me that the theft of the horses was somehow connected to one or both of the recent deaths – Doyle Crouch and Fiona McBride. Grady had known them. Could he throw some light on this?

Though uncertain, I was inclined to believe that Ross McConnell contributed to Fiona's fall and might therefore be responsible for her death. But who could I report this to? Certainly not Ross.

I looked Grady in the eye. "I'd like to see you again, but honestly, I won't be in Ireland long. Still, if you'd like to hang out, I wish you'd help me find those horses."

"Then I think we should start by locating O'Malley. Rumor is he may still be alive."

I didn't want to disclose what I knew about that yet. "I agree," I said, "but first, I'd like to check the flight records at Shannon Airport on the day the horses were flown to the U.S. Would that be possible?"

"An acquaintance of mine has replaced Doyle Crouch until a permanent inspector is appointed. Since I'm a regular customer, that should be no problem. What time shall I pick you up?"

I was surprised, yet pleased, with his positive response. Grady Quinn was a good man but be careful, I thought.

"Nine in the morning would work. Afterwards, let me buy lunch." I said. "I owe you."

He held my hand and bent to kiss my cheek. Impulsively, I turned and pressed by lips to his. His mouth was full and firm. He tasted good, and I was slow to back away. Despite the rain, his face smelled of intriguing after shave – reminded me of dad's favorite, *Stetson*.

"Right....well....we'll discuss lunch later," he said with the surprise of the kiss still in his eyes.

"Thanks for everything," I said. "I'll never match that ride with Clancy and the Blazers." If a girl ever needed a gentle protector, this was her man.

"'Twas my pleasure." He slipped on his cap, pulled open the front door, turned up his collar and, like Bogie, disappeared into the Irish mist.

21

The receptionist handed me the key to my room, wrapped in a slip of paper. "Miss Porter, you received this overseas call while you were hunting."

As I walked down the hall, I was stunned by the message. "P.J., come home immediately. Your horse is dying. Father."

I felt lightheaded and braced myself against the wall. I should have flown home two days ago – the moment I'd learned of the Copperhead bite. I wasn't obligated to Kit Devereux to try to clear O'Malley, and the reward money for finding the horses wasn't worth compromising my loyalty to Transport.

When I returned to the room, I called the front desk for Aer Lingus's number. I needed to immediately make a reservation to Oklahoma City. Before dialing, I examined the note again. Something didn't ring true. My father would not wait until Transport was dying to contact me. Our agreement was that he was to call if there was a turn for the worse, giving me ample time to fly home. And I doubt he would refer to me as "P.J" and to himself as "Father." Between us, I was always "Parker" and he was "Dad."

Instead of the airline, I called home. "Dad, how's Transport?"

"About the same. Dr. Jett is planning to operate in a few hours. We've got our fingers crossed. How are you?" he asked.

"I'm fine. Did you call me today?"

"No, why?" he asked.

I knew it. Someone was jerking my chain – or, more accurately, twisting my arm to drop the inquiry.

"There must have been a mix-up in room messages," I said. "Not important, Dad."

"When are you coming home?" he asked.

"It'll be a couple more days, unless things don't go well with Transport. Dad, you'd telephone immediately if anything goes wrong, right?"

"Of course! And I'll call you with the results of the surgery."

"Thanks. Got to run, Dad. Love you. Bye for now."

"Love you, too, Parker. Goodbye."

I sat on the edge of the bed. The night maid had placed more chocolates on my pillow. I savored the milky flavor – it helped me think.

Who wanted me out of town? I wouldn't rule out McConnell – but he was hunting with the Blazers when the call came in. Could he have a deputy or associate doing his dirty work?

Since I'm the only outsider who knows O'Malley's alive, could it have been O'Malley himself, or maybe his cousin, Frank Reilly, the night manager? But O'Malley had proposed the meeting with me and seemed to sincerely want my help. Maybe everything changed once he learned that Doyle Crouch was dead. But why?"

And what about Grady Quinn? I was becoming close to him, even about to confide that O'Malley was alive. Could he have me fooled? Might he be associated with one of these other characters? Maybe his assignment was to keep me distracted.

I popped another chocolate. Is it possible this thing involved more than stolen horses? I needed to brainstorm the facts with someone else. Picking up the phone, I lay back on the bed and called Simon.

I could hear someone jostling the phone. "It's Parker. We need to talk." I said.

"Hey, I'm asleep – or was asleep," he said in groggy voice. "What time is it? Never mind! Give me a minute, will ya?" Then I could hear running water in the background as if he was splashing his face.

Returning to the phone, he asked, "Are you okay? You sound upset."

"I'm fine – maybe stressed. Sorry to interrupt your beauty rest, but there are some new wrinkles," I said. Then starting with the ominous phone message from someone posing as my father, I brought him up to date, including my mistrust of Sergeant McConnell and the mysterious deaths of Fiona McBride and Doyle Crouch. I also informed him of my plan, with the help of Grady Quinn, to examine the flight records at Shannon Airport in the morning. I left out that I was uneasy because I still had misgivings about Quinn – mainly uncertain personal feelings.

Usually, Simon had practical advice, but this time, nothing, just a hair-pulling suggestion. "P.J., sounds like you're on to something. Just stay the course. You'll figure it out."

I rolled my eyes. "Is that all you've got for me?" I asked.

"Sorry. But you're there and I'm here and it's late."

I nodded and sighed. "You're right." I needed to step back, calm down and continue sifting through the evidence.

Resigned to the fact that he couldn't solve my problems, I asked, "Anything new with you?"

"Well, I changed semesters at Georgetown and caught the *red eye* home. So we'll be studying together after all. I know you'll be excited about that. And the Farrells' private jet is picking me up at Wiley Post Airport tomorrow morning and flying me to Dallas. They're putting me up in their *hacienda*, and we'll be reviewing everything."

"While you're with the Farrells, there's something else you should think about," I said.

"What's that?"

"I can't ask Sergeant McConnell for help to access the records of the New York Animal Import Center – I no longer trust him. You're going to have to figure that out from your end."

"Let me work on it. I think the Farrells should be able to help. I'll keep you posted."

"Simon, I have a feeling this case involves more than I first thought. Maybe more players. Two people are dead, and someone's trying to get me out of Dodge. So you be careful!"

"You too, P.J. And by the way, I miss you."

"Likewise. Goodnight, partner," I said. It was difficult to be romantic when he was three thousand miles away, and I had so much on my plate.

* * * * * * *

I had a restless night. Between the bogus phone message and anticipation of the drive to Shannon with Grady, mixed with confused feelings for Grady and Simon, how could I sleep at all?

At dawn, I dressed and went down to the lobby. No one was around. I suppose Frank Reilly was snoozing in his private office. Two samovars of fresh coffee with a pitcher of whole cream and a bowl of cane sugar were beside the front door for early risers. I was surprised that I was ahead of the morning walkers and joggers. Fixing a mug of steaming French Roast, I stepped outside into the silent fog.

I could barely see the outlines of the horses across the bar ditch. They seemed to be huddled together, maybe to keep warm. I whistled, hoping Clancy would come forward for a morning greeting. I strolled to the edge of the ditch but still couldn't pick him out. Then I realized that the herd had surrounded something on the ground, as if posting guard. Squinting, I could make out that it was one of the horses. Oh no – it was Clancy – he was down! Yesterday's stressful conditions must have caused him to colic.

If he had coliced, it was crucial that he get up and move about to clear his intestines. I yelled across, "Clancy, rise and shine!"

No reaction. But not unusual – colicky horses can slip into a stupor.

I climbed down into the canal, waded through a foot of muddy water and scrambled up the slick bank. The other horses moved aside.

"Clancy!" I shouted again. "Wake up! On your feet, boy!" Still no response.

I leaned down to stroke his neck. Then I saw it. A small hole above his right eye with blood oozing from the rim. Beautiful Clancy had been shot. "Oh, my God!" I covered his nose – breathless and cold. Who would kill such a gorgeous animal? I shook my fist in anger and sobbed.

Then I noticed something white protruding from one of his ears – a folded piece of paper. How cruel. I lifted it and read, "P.J. Porter has twenty-four hours to get out of Ireland, or she's next."

I staggered to my knees. "Clancy – Clancy – this is all my fault!" Tears streamed down my face, and the droplets settled on his stilled face.

22

I LAY DOWN ON MY BED IN OKLAHOMA CITY, CLOSED MY EYES AND PICTURED P.J. On the phone, she'd sounded overwhelmed. I knew a lot of that pressure stemmed from her ailing horse. She was torn between pursuing the investigation and returning home to comfort Transport.

Something else concerned me – P.J. didn't sound like she'd missed me or had even been thinking of me. Whatever happened to *absence makes the heart grow fonder*?

Officer P.J. Porter and I'd first met in Oklahoma City at Trails End Stables, an equestrian center that catered to talented young riders from affluent families. A member of the Trails End team, socialite Selina Norman, a champion show jumper, was suspiciously killed in a harrowing riding accident. She was fun and gorgeous and a world class athlete, and I was her lowly show groom.

P.J., two years out of the Police Academy, was

assigned to assist in the inquiry. We began to share information, and within days, I'd become her unofficial partner.

Once we'd unraveled the Trails End mystery, the *Oklahoma Tribune* referred to us as "gifted sleuths," who had solved *The Mink and Manure Murders*.

A week later, P.J. and I were contacted by the Duke of Grantham in Leicestershire, England. He persuaded us to be his guest at story-book Grantham Castle and infiltrate the Royal Society for the Prevention of Cruelty to Animals. The object was to expose a murderer and the source of widespread violence directed at foxhunts and their officials.

We proved to ourselves and the people of Leicestershire that we were no fluke but an authentic crime-solving team. In the process, we experienced a unique adventure, sampling the exclusive lifestyle of English aristocracy and riding fabulous horses over spectacular countryside, all while lining our pockets with coin of the realm.

In uniform, P.J. was savvy and by the book. Out of uniform, either in jeans and boots, or classy evening attire, she was a knockout but always cool with her wits about her. It baffles me how I've been able to keep my hands off this woman.

And therein lies the rub. When we first met, she suspected I was in love with Selina. I might have been infatuated, but love – I'm not sure. During both cases, P.J. and I worked well together, but we had to curb our sexual impulses. One lapse ended in a roll in the hay, actually, under a luxurious down comforter, in romantic Grantham Castle. But, to continue as partners, we had to resolve to keep our libidos in check.

Now that P.J. was in Ireland, everything except the investigation was on hold. I'd concluded she was more my type than Selina. Still, to make a permanent commitment – I wasn't quite ready.

P.J. and I planned to attend Georgetown Law School, starting in three months. I considered suggesting a live-in arrangement while we were in Washington but feared she might overreact and break off our relationship. I couldn't risk that. What our future held was unclear. Nothing to do but back off, focus on the inquiry and hope time would resolve our feelings.

23

Tex Farrell had instructed me to be in the private plane lounge at Oklahoma City's Wiley Post Airport at 10 a.m. I would be met by one of his pilots.

At five minutes after, a slender young woman, dressed in a slate blue uniform with matching captain's cap and sporting navy and white cowboy boots, approached me. "John Simon Rush?"

I nodded

"I'm Maureen Farrell, Tex's daughter – your co-pilot to Dallas. Are you ready to board?"

I hesitated, struck by her snug attire, her steady blue eyes and how that mass of strawberry blonde hair had been stuffed into her little space-cadet cap. She reminded me of a James Bond *femme fatale*.

"Yes, ma'am," I replied, jumping to my feet and grabbing my duffle.

"May I check your identification, please?"

"Certainly." I fumbled through my jeans and

produced my driver's license.

She studied it, glancing back and forth to make sure there was a match. Overly officious for a private flight, I thought.

"Sorry about that. If I'm caught ignoring that FAA rule, I might lose my pilot's license."

"I understand." I shouldn't have been so cynical.

"Follow me. The captain's running the checklist. We should be good to go."

About fifty yards away, a glistening torpedo-shaped Gulfstream was parked on the tarmac. Scrolled along its side, in big powder blue letters, outlined in black, was *Far-L Ranch*.

"Are you a detective, Mr. Rush?" She asked as we strolled toward the aircraft.

"Call me Simon, please."

"I'm Maureen."

I nodded. "Actually, I'm a prospective law student who dabbles in detective work. P.J. Porter's a police officer. We're a team. I'm sure your father explained that she's in Ireland."

"Yes, I've heard about P.J. and your partnership." Did I detect a note of skepticism?

We boarded the jet through a narrow hatch. "That's our pilot, Josh Logan," Maureen said, pointing into the cockpit.

A rugged looking man, probably in his fifties, peered around the corner, extending his hand.

"Welcome aboard, Mr. Rush. Tighten your seat belt – might be a few rough spots today. But we'll be fine."

I shook his hand. He had a strong grip which gave me confidence. "Nice to be here – look forward to the ride. And I'm good at following orders."

Both Josh and Maureen chuckled which lightened the mood.

I selected a plush armchair toward the front. I'd heard how convenient private planes were, but I had no idea they were this luxurious. The interior, including the floors, seats and ceiling, were decorated in color coordinated fabrics and leather with mahogany trim. Two words came to mind – shamelessly excessive. The other ten or so seats were conspicuously empty.

Maureen made sure I was buckled in. "Though it's a short trip, don't move about without asking."

I nodded.

Then she took her place in the cockpit, and within minutes, we were airborne.

Once we'd leveled off at 15,000 feet, she returned to the cabin. "Can I offer you something to drink, Simon?"

"Black coffee, if it's not too much trouble."

She opened two cabinet doors, pulled a lever and, within seconds, presented me with a carafe of coffee and monogrammed mug.

"That was quick. Thank you."

"Compliments of Far-L airline," she said. "We

usually offer Bloody Marys, but we're out of vodka at the moment."

"No problem. I prefer coffee in the morning, anyway."

"Good."

She settled into the opposite chair and tilted back her cap. "Do you or your partner have any idea, yet, how our horses were stolen or where they might be?"

"Not yet, but we're confident we'll turn up some leads. P.J.'s been interviewing the people involved in the sale and transport of your animals. Her next step is to examine the flight records at Shannon Airport, particularly important since the government inspector, who authorized the shipping of the horses, has mysteriously turned up dead."

She seemed unconcerned about the inspector's demise, only that we had no information about her horses.

"I see. What do you expect to learn from my father?" she asked, changing the subject.

I sidestepped this for the moment. "Several things....Were you at your ranch when the horses arrived?"

She shook her head. "I was at a horse show in Houston."

"Well, I'd like to get your father's take on the transport agent who delivered the horses and check the documents that accompanied them. I'd also like to meet with the vet who examined the animals."

"We can arrange all that," she said with a slight frown.

Why wasn't she more anxious to assist me?

At that moment, the plane bounced as we hit a stretch of turbulence. Maureen turned toward the cockpit. "Do you need me up there, Josh?" she asked the pilot.

"I've got it. When I need you, I'll holler."

Turning back to me, she asked, "From the papers, we thought we'd received the authentic horses 'til I rode them."

"I hadn't heard that," I said.

"As soon as I trotted some polls and popped over a few rails, I knew they were frauds – no way were they Grand Prix quality. Do you ride, Simon?"

"I do. As a matter fact, I own a Grand Prix jumper," I boasted.

"Anyone I've ever seen or heard of on the circuit?"

"Maybe. He's a big Holsteiner named My Hero."

Her face beamed. "Sure. Wasn't that Selina Norman's ride? She competed with him all over the Southwest."

"That's the one. I bought him. You knew Selina died?"

She nodded. "Everyone did – happened in Ft. Worth – terrible tragedy. Do you show My Hero?"

"I'm not in that league," I said, shaking my head.

"Besides, I don't have the time or money. I'd like to partner with a professional to compete him. Hero needs to continue what he was bred to do."

Her eyes lit up. "I agree! Simon, I'm a pro, and I'd like to explore that with you. I had high hopes for those Irish horses, but now –"

At that moment, the plane must have dropped fifty feet. It felt as though the bottom had fallen out. My mug and decanter flew into space. As Maureen stumbled toward the cockpit, we hit another air pocket, and her head banged against the ceiling. I grabbed her jacket to steady her. She staggered back, collapsing in my lap, stunned but still conscious. Her thick hair and cap had probably cushioned the impact.

She looked around at me, dazed, and our faces touched, cheek grazing cheek. Her glossed mouth brushed my temple, and her hair covered my eyes. It smelled like – fresh wheat.

Seconds passed while we anticipated another jolt. "Are you all right, Maureen?" I asked.

"I think so." She held her head as she staggered to her feet. She had the same tall, athletic frame as P.J. which I found irresistible.

Josh turned and peered into our cabin. "Everybody okay?"

"We're fine," she mumbled, still slightly confused.

"Maureen, better give me a hand up here! Dallas wants us to climb a thousand feet. We've got some serious storm-dodging ahead."

"Coming," she said, shaking out the cobwebs.

Fortunate that P.J. wasn't along. With her phobia of flying and me playing kissy-face with the co-pilot, she'd be throwing a fit.

24

An hour later, we landed, not at Love Field in Dallas as I expected, but on a narrow strip of pavement at the Far-L Ranch.

During the approach, I scanned the sunbaked, open range below. The land was pockmarked with hundreds, maybe thousands, of tiny blemishes. Being from Oklahoma, I knew what those zits were – oil and gas wells. Not far from the runway was an expanse of irrigated green, dotted with a sprawling ranch house and five barns or stables. Three riding arenas and numerous holding pastures were spread out beyond the buildings. This was a serious horse operation.

As the luggage was being unloaded, I spotted a lanky man in cowboy hat and boots, sporting an oversized silver belt buckle that glittered in the morning sun. He was standing beside a white limousine, waiving to us. It had to be Tex Farrell.

"Welcome, Mr. Rush," he said. He gave me a

vigorous shake with a massive, calloused hand, then effortlessly tossed my duffle into the trunk.

"Dad, he goes by 'Simon,'" Maureen corrected.

"Remind me if I forget, will you, son?" He spoke with an ingratiating drawl.

"Yes, sir, I can do that."

"And you call me Tex or anything that suits you," he said, giving me a friendly pat in the shoulder.

I smiled. "Tex it is."

He had a long, weathered face to match his hands. I'm six feet two, and Tex was nearly a head taller. I could see that Maureen had inherited his blue eyes and height. She was probably five foot eleven.

My quick assessment of Tex Farrell, mainly from his wry grin and discerning eyes, was that he was a *good ol' boy*, who could skin you alive in a business deal. Maureen seemed to possess the same keen wit.

Once we were settled in the limo, Tex suggested, "Let's have a bite to eat at the house. Then, Simon, you and Maureen can look at the horses. I've arranged for our vet, Dr. Pedro Manuel, he goes by "Dr. Pete," to meet you at the barn. Sound okay?"

"That's fine. I appreciate you and Maureen making these arrangements."

He nodded. "Our pleasure, son. We want to help. Maureen's convinced the Irish horses can be found – I'm not so sure."

There was one delicate matter I was anxious to settle

before we did anything further. "Tex, if it's okay, P.J. Porter and I would like to clarify our arrangement with you – get that out of the way."

"Good idea," Maureen said. "Business before pleasure."

Tex's eyes narrowed. "Let's hear it, son."

I nodded. "We're prepared to try to find the horses you purchased from Sean O'Malley in Ireland under these conditions: If we're successful, you'll pay us the published reward of one hundred thousand dollars. And you agree to pay the full amount even if anyone in the Farrell family, including Maureen, contribute to a successful outcome. Are we in agreement here?"

"Son, you talk like a lawyer. But you're right, that's the deal. And we Farrells will stand behind it. Right, Maureen?"

Her mouth tightened. "One thing, though," she said. "I don't think we should be expected to pay if the horses are found dead. They'd be no use to us, then."

I looked at Tex, but his poker face revealed nothing.

My mind raced. P.J. and I couldn't afford to spend our valuable time and end up with the short end of the stick.

"I can't agree to that!" I exclaimed. "If we're to use our expertise to find these animals, we have to be paid whether they're dead or alive! Otherwise, we could spend a lot of time, and you wouldn't be out a nickel."

Maureen appeared irritated and uncompromising, then looked at her father. Tex lowered his head for a moment then nodded. Maureen, still frowning, said, "All right. That's the deal."

I repressed a grin but wished P.J. were here to pat me on the back.

Tex tilted his hat. "Agreed, but I want it on record that I hate the way you lawyers bargain."

Maureen's face finally relaxed into a smile. "Oh, Dad. Think of all the trouble we lawyers have gotten you out of." She obviously had her father wrapped around her finger.

Tex frowned. "Yeh, you've got a point."

* * * * * * *

The Farrell ranch house was about fifteen thousand square feet of western extravagance with a circular drive wide enough for four vehicles. Construction was a combination of gray rock and white frame with a columned porte-cochere that struggled to give it southern charm.

We entered the main living area, adequate in size to host a polo match. My suspicion was that while the Farrells were vacationing in the Bahamas, an upscale decorator had gone wild in here with cowhide, steer horns and polished mesquite.

A swarthy man with a black ponytail, wearing a leather vest and string tie, appeared from nowhere and took my bag.

Tex pointed toward one of four hallways leading off the living room. "Simon, follow Cal, wash up, then meet us on the patio."

My bedroom was a mix of exotic Southwestern and Mexican décor. The bedposts of the overstuffed, kingsize bed were made from the horns of Texas steers. The four walls of the bathroom, as well as the ceiling, were covered with Mexican tiles, and the coordinated twin sinks and tub on legs were hand-painted porcelain.

"Patio" was an understatement. The covered veranda ran the full length of the house and overlooked a Polynesian swimming complex. Since there were no God-made mountains or waterfalls in the background, the Farrells had created their own around two swimming pools, the entire complex enclosed by an eight-foot-high glass wind guard. Within it, a south sea paradise had been laid out with palm trees, palmettos, flowering cacti and pink bougainvilleas. The effect was spectacular.

While Cal served a light lunch of thin-sliced, barbequed brisket, beans and coleslaw, Tex spread out the documents that had arrived with the counterfeit horses. He slid one of the passports toward me. "Look here," he said, pointing to the various markings. "This is Rock of Cashel's. It shows a diamond-shaped blaze on his forehead and a white sock on the left fore. All this matches the chestnut we received. But when we studied the video and some snapshots, we saw that the real Rocky had a star-shaped blaze and only a trace of a sock. Other than that, the phony horse was a decent look-alike. During shipping, no one picked up on that, but then, why should they? The markings matched the phony papers."

I looked closely at the two passports. "I've seen a number of these, and they look authentic," I said. "It's a very professional forgery. We'll need to determine where they were made, maybe from the quality of paper or the printing."

Maureen's expression changed to condescending. "We've done that. Dad has a connection with the F.B.I. in Dallas. I showed them the passports. Washington said they were probably German made but offered nothing more."

She acted like she'd done the research I should have. Was she expecting a tip?

I ignored her attitude and concentrated on my delicious meal and the surroundings. I'm a barbecue gourmet, and the lunch, served on oversized hand-painted Mexican platters, was superior to any I'd ever eaten. While we ate, Tex explained with obvious pride that the south sea theme of the swimming area had been Maureen's vision, but the outrageous expense of constructing it was his contribution. He seemed on the verge of disclosing the exact dollar amount, but Maureen dissuaded him with a kick to the shin which rocked the table. There seemed to be a hard side to Maureen that said *be careful.*

After washing down honeyed *sopaipillas* with coffee, Tex rose to leave. "Sorry, but I have work to do. Maureen will take it from here. We'll talk more at dinner."

I attempted to rise, but he placed his strong hand

on my shoulder. "Stay put, son. We're not formal 'round here."

"Tex, thanks for everything, especially the plane ride," I said. "That made getting here quick and easy."

He patted me on the back. "Our pleasure," he said. "Good luck with your search."

Maureen and I sat quietly for a moment. Finally, I asked, "Did I understand you're a lawyer?"

She ran her hand through her pile of reddish blonde hair in an almost flirtatious gesture. "Not exactly," she said. "I'm a graduate of the University of Virginia Law School and a member of the Texas Bar, but I've never practiced. Someday I'll inherit this ranch, so Dad thought law school would come in handy. How 'bout you?"

"I'll be a freshmen at Georgetown Law in January."

"You're getting a late start, aren't you?"

I agreed, but I didn't need that from her.

I nodded. "I was a ranch manager in Wyoming for several years, but things happened, and my life changed course."

Maureen leaned closer. "Did the new direction have anything to do with Selina Norman's death? I read about how you solved her murder."

I resented her prying and looked away. Cal was standing on the edge of the patio, waiting to clear the table. "Aren't we supposed to meet the vet?" I asked.

"Selina's obviously a sensitive subject. At some point, though, I want to talk to you about My Hero. I have some ideas. But that will keep," she said, pushing back from the table. Maureen rose to leave, twisting her hair into a ponytail which she slipped through the back of her ball cap.

When we arrived at the barn, Dr. Pete climbed out of a 4 x 4 Chevy Silverado. The barn was one of the buildings I'd seen from the air – light green steel outlined with natural cedar, and immaculately maintained. The vet was short, wore a cowboy hat and boots and tinted glasses. His dark complexion confirmed he was not only of Mexican descent but was accustomed to making house calls in sunny pastures. He led us to where the horses were stalled, threw halters over their heads and tied them up outside so we could have a good look.

I was impressed with the counterfeit horses. They appeared fit and well cared for. Considerable planning had gone into locating such credible substitutes.

"Dr. Pete, let me ask you something," I said, patting the gray's back. "Tex pointed out the marking differences between the fraudulent horses and the real ones. When you examined these substitute horses, did you find anything else that looked out of order?"

"Well, yes, I did. This one has a white sock on his right rear. That ankle had traces of gray dye – like someone wanted to cover up the white."

I rubbed his leg, but nothing came off. "The thief probably thought he could dye the fake animals to match the real horses then decided it would be easier to create fraudulent passports. Anything else?"

"Well, yes. Small areas on the necks of both horses had been recently rubbed with an oily salve."

I examined the gray's neck. There was still residue of a quarter-sized mark forward of the shoulder, near the mane. That seemed odd. If it was a liniment or coat conditioner, why not rub the entire neck or, at least, a larger area?

I turned to the vet. "Did you have it analyzed?"

He nodded. "Give me a minute." He hustled to his truck and returned with a notebook. "The lab said it primarily contained Shark liver oil and Phenylephrine. Nothing harmful."

I recognized those elements and had to chuckle. We used an oddball treatment at Trails End Stables that contained identical ingredients. "Aren't those the basic components in a common over-the-counter medication?" I asked.

Dr. Pete scowled. "I don't know. What would that be?"

I smiled smugly. "Preparation H."

Maureen shrugged. "Simon, what in the world are you talking about?"

"Where have you guys been?" I joked. "In Oklahoma, it's a popular astringent used to heal cuts and bites on horses. It also contains Vitamin A which promotes rapid hair growth."

She shook her head. "Okay, we've never heard of it used on horses. So what? There were no cuts or marks on their necks."

I couldn't resist. "Of course not! That's because the stuff works!"

Maureen was not amused. "Enough with the jokes – tell us what's going on here."

Savoring the moment, I paused and tapped the oily stain with my finger. "If we had a microchip scanner, I'd bet anything we'd find an implant directly below this spot. Preparation H was probably used to seal and quickly cover the incision. And this could tell us something else, maybe important."

Maureen folded her arms. "We can hardly wait," she said.

"As a horse medication, I've never heard of it being used outside the Southwest. Competitors from the East that I've met at shows laughed when I recommended it. So I'd wager anything it hasn't found its way across the pond."

She shifted her stance and stared at Dr. Pete.

* * * * * * *

Once we'd put up the horses and thanked the vet for his time, Maureen and I ambled down the gravel road toward the house. I sensed she was wrestling with the implications of the unorthodox use of Preparation H.

Finally, she asked, "Are you thinking what I am?"

"What's that?"

"If Preparation H is not known overseas as an equine

astringent, the microchip switch from Rock of Cashel and Resident Magistrate must have been performed here. This suggests that the real horses could be stashed here in the U.S., not in Ireland or Europe as we've been thinking. Right?"

I nodded. Despite her mean-spirited disposition, I welcomed Maureen's input. She was no P.J., but I might need her as a sounding board.

"That crossed my mind," I said. "And there's something else that bothers me. How were the microchips removed from the genuine animals without endangering their performance as show horses? Neck muscle damage could render them worthless. The thieves must have come up with a unique technique."

Maureen stared at me, as if waiting for a brilliant explanation, but, at the moment, I had none.

Adjusting her cap, she said, "More for you to investigate. Meantime, maybe you can enlighten me on something else."

"I'll try," I said.

"When horses are shipped internationally, I thought only passports were required by law. What about microchips? Are they necessary, and do they have to be verified?"

P.J. and I had checked this out. "Only passports are required by law and must be inspected when leaving Ireland and again upon arrival at Kennedy and at the New York Animal Import Center. Microchips, though optional, have become more prevalent, and it's customary to scan them at the time passports are checked. Which reminds me, Maureen, did you or your father review the records at Kennedy International?"

Maureen's face flushed. "We left all that to the transport agent – the guy that moved them from Kennedy to the Animal Import Center at Rock Tavern. We never heard that anything was wrong."

I was surprised the Farrells hadn't been more thorough. "I'd like to check the records at Kennedy, but I'm not sure how to gain access."

Maureen nodded. "I think you *should* examine those." She paused a moment then coyly smiled. "Tell you what. I'll make you a trade-off you can't refuse."

I grinned. "This should be good. Let's hear it."

"The Far-L plane goes to New York on Monday, day after tomorrow. I'll fly you there on one condition."

"What's the catch?" I asked.

"Tomorrow, you and I drive to Chandler, Oklahoma and take a look at My Hero. If he's as good as I think, I'll make you a proposition."

Her flirtatious smirk reminded me of P.J. "I assume this proposition concerns Hero, not me?"

"Don't flatter yourself, big boy."

25

As the sun was breaking the horizon, we tore through a gate framed with hundreds of steer horns, and headed north for Chandler, Oklahoma, three and a half hours away. Maureen reminded me of a Levi model – tight jeans, lizard boots and her long ponytail floating behind her denim cap.

Since she'd forewarned me that, regardless of weather, we'd make the trip in her turquoise Mercedes with the top down, I wore a sweater and loose windbreaker borrowed from Tex, and aviator sunglasses.

The night before, I'd telephoned Dr. Guy Porter, P.J.'s father, at the family farm in Chandler where I boarded Hero. Though he worked at Oklahoma State's College of Veterinary Medicine at Stillwater, he usually spent weekends at the homestead, forty miles from his office. I explained who Maureen was and her interest in Hero. He planned to be at the farm most of the day.

"Simon, if you and Miss Farrell wanted to ride out together, you're welcome to try Cargo, Parker's young horse. He needs the exercise. But I wouldn't jump him

– he's too green." I remembered Cargo when P.J. and I introduced him to the turbulent stream on the Porter spread. He became so excited he slipped and fell, dunking P.J. in an icy pool.

"Thank you. We'll think about that. How's Transport?" I asked.

"I assume you know about the snake bite?"

"P.J.'s kept me up to date."

"He's just had surgery to remove gangrenous tissue around his ankle. Unfortunately, that turned out to be more extensive than Dr. Jett thought. As soon as his system settles, he'll need a skin graft to protect the tendons. Bottom line, Transport's still fighting for his life."

"Sorry to hear that, but I'll hold good thoughts. I know P.J.'s been very worried."

I was concerned, maybe selfishly, that she'd decide to drop everything and come home, just as we were getting started. Bad timing because it had become clearer to me how important the reward money would be for law school.

"I'm about to phone her," he said. "Do you have anything for me to pass along?"

"Just tell her I'll be calling in a day or so." In private, I planned on reporting the Preparation H saga and anything we learned from the Kennedy records. Now the biggie would be to explain why I'd brought Maureen to P.J.'s family home without discussing it with her first. That could be a problem.

IRISH MIST

* * * * * * *

Maureen drove the same way she flew the Gulfstream – fast.

"Your family may be able to fix speeding tickets in Texas," I said, "but the Oklahoma Highway Patrol won't be so forgiving – and they're thick as flies once you cross that state line. They even have helicopter spotters."

She glanced at me and smiled. "Ha! How'd you know about my tickets?" she joked. "Okay, you're right. There's no hurry." She slowed from eighty-five to seventy-five, just five miles over the limit, and I eased back into the plush leather seat.

"That's more like it," I sighed.

She tuned in some soft, country-western on the radio. Finally, she asked, "How did you acquire Hero?"

I explained how Selina's grandparents, her executors, wanted to give Hero to me for helping solve Selina's death. Her parents had been killed in a plane accident when she was young. Anyway, I ended up purchasing Hero for a nominal amount.

"So you've owned him for three or four months. Who's been riding him?"

"Just me, but not often – I live thirty miles away. I've probably been on him once a week since we moved him to Chandler. But he's turned out every day, so that helps. Still, I know that's not enough exercise for a powerful Holsteiner, accustomed to being ridden five to six times a week and jumped two or more. I've been trying to figure out what to do with him."

She patted my arm. "That's where I come in, my friend. First, I need to check him out – pop him over a few rails. Can I do that at the Porter farm?"

"We'll see. There're a few jumps in a small arena behind the barn that might work," I replied.

* * * * * * *

The most impressive thing about the white, clapboard Porter home, other than the Victorian wraparound porch, was that the core of the house was built in 1907, the same year as Oklahoma achieved statehood. Equally interesting was that, forty years later, almost to the day, oil was discovered on the four hundred acres and was still producing.

Dr. Porter was coming down the front steps when we pulled in. "How was the drive?" he asked, pumping my hand.

"No problems and no tickets," I joked, smiling at Maureen. "Dr. Porter, this is Maureen Farrell."

She surprised me by greeting him with a vigorous hand shake and a knockout smile. "I believe we've met before, Dr. Porter. Two years ago, my father and I delivered a palomino Quarter Horse to your Vet Med clinic for colic surgery."

"Sure, I remember. Your father's a tall fellow, right?"

"Yes, sir, very tall."

"Well, I'm pleased to meet you. Simon, I apologize, but there's been a medical emergency at the Vet Med in Stillwater. You'll be on your own. Both Hero and Cargo are still turned out. If you're going to ride, you'll have to catch them. Carrots are in a bucket in the barn."

He tilted his soiled hat. "You're welcome to stay the night if you run late – there's plenty of food and beer in the refrig. Key's in the hanging flower pot. Make yourselves at home – and I mean it!" I thought the corners of his mouth faintly turned up.

He reached for Maureen's hand. "I'm sorry to leave so abruptly, but there always seems to be a crisis."

"We understand," I said, "and we'll make sure everything's locked up. Should we leave the horses in their stalls when we go or turn them out?"

"Stalls would be fine. Buck, our foreman, will check their water and give them evening grain." With that he pulled down his hat and climbed in the pickup.

As he was about to drive off, I had an afterthought. I ran toward his truck, waving. He braked to a dusty stop and rolled down the window. My query concerned microchips implanted in the necks of horses. For security reasons, I assumed they were manufactured by a high-tech, patented process that would be impossible to duplicate. When I asked Dr. Porter, I was surprised he didn't know, but he promised to consult certain O.S.U. professors and get back to me.

It had occurred to me that if Rock of Cashel's and

Resident Magistrate's implants could be duplicated, dangerous switching surgery would be unnecessary. The copied chips could be inserted in the usual way with a syringe, anywhere, any time. However, there was a glitch. What if the fraudulent horses already had their own implanted chips? That would present another complication – more surgery – more risk – more opportunity for suspicion and detention.

Once Dr. Porter drove off, Maureen asked, "What was that all about?"

"I asked him where the key to the tack room was. We're going to need saddles and bridles."

This was a lie, but the Farrells couldn't be ruled out as suspects just because Maureen was a stunner and her father a good ol' boy. The real horses might be hidden on the Far-L Ranch in one of their fancy barns. When the dust settled, maybe they intended to collect the insurance money, then further profit from a sale – probably overseas – Dubai came to mind. Experience told me to proceed with caution – anything was possible.

"Let's find those carrots and catch some horses," I said.

* * * * * * *

From the trunk of her car, Maureen gathered up her hard hat, gloves and a protective vest.

"Do you have other boots?" I asked.

Her eyes narrowed with disdain. "These cowboy boots are fine."

I questioned this, but shut up. The long heels might be locked in the stirrups in the event of a jumping fall.

We strolled down the gravel path toward the neat, eight-stall barn. Maureen surprised me with a friendly slap on the shoulder. "I'm excited about trying Hero!" she said. "I remember in Houston when he intimidated the other competitors just by his proud presence. Simon, fate has brought us together – I can feel it. Can't you?"

"Ha! Why don't you test ride him before we involve fate?"

We each grabbed a halter, along with a handful of carrots and headed for the pasture, fifty yards away. Hero and Cargo raised their handsome heads to study us as we climbed through the white post-and-rail fence.

"Come on, fellas! Look what we have." I called. Hero's eyes widened, and he whinnied. Cargo froze in his stance and stared suspiciously. Before I could decide on our next move, Hero galloped toward us, and Cargo followed. They charged to a dust-churning halt, close enough to have their noses scratched. I flattered myself that Hero'd missed me and was not confusing me with Selina. I slid a carrot in the side of his mouth, and he nuzzled my shoulder.

"He's gorgeous!" Maureen said, admiring Hero while stroking and feeding Cargo. "How old is he?"

"Nearly nine. Here, I'll take Cargo." When we switched, Hero shook his head as if to say, *Hey! What's going on? You're my friend and master. Who's this stranger?* I couldn't resist a smile of satisfaction.

As we led the horses back to the barn, I pointed to the other side. "The ring's over there. Let's leave Cargo in his stall, and I'll set rails for you. If we have time, we can trail ride. Sound okay?" I asked.

"Work's for me," she replied.

The small oval-shaped arena contained three adjustable jumps – one on the near side and two more, a stride apart, on the other. I doubted that Maureen could evaluate Hero's Grand Prix potential in this limited space, but we'd see.

"You ever jumped him here?" she asked.

"No, just cross country, over a few logs." I'd never considered anything bigger because there was seldom anyone else around.

She frowned. "Well, it's over three months then since he's been jumped in an enclosure. That may be too long for a real test."

Once we'd saddled Hero, Maureen led him around the ring by the reins to acquaint him with the obstacles and the enclosing post-and-rail fence. Occasionally, she'd pause in front of a jump to assure him this was not a difficult course. Then he'd glance at me. I'd nod, and she'd speak to him softly. "This is a piece of cake for you, boy. Nothing to it." She had a gentle way, and I watched Hero relax and gain confidence.

The walking around and whispering sweet nothings

continued for twenty minutes. Finally, Maureen said, "I think we're ready. Would you mind holding his head?"

I grasped Hero's bridle. "Need a leg up?"

"That won't be necessary." Her tone said I should know better. What's this gal's problem? Too proud to accept a little help?

Holding the reins in her left hand, she raised her left foot high into the stirrup, coiled her lower back to the breaking point, then swung aboard with the fluid motion of gymnast. Impressive. I never would have tried that on a seventeen hand horse without a mounting block – too hard on the sacroiliac.

She collected the reins and shifted in the saddle to let Hero know it was time to work. They appeared well proportioned. Hero studied me as they moved off at the walk.

"Don't you have a crop?" I asked. "Selina always rode him with one. I never saw her use it – just an authority thing."

"I didn't bring a whip. Could you find one?" she asked.

I pointed toward the barn. "Give me a minute."

I squeezed through the fence and jogged off. Hero neighed at the top of his lungs. *Hey! Where are you going? Don't leave me alone with this broad.* I loved that horse.

As I snatched one of the crops from a hook, I heard Maureen scream. "Whoa! Hey, whoa!" Then, "You son of a bitch, whoa!" Followed by silence.

I raced back toward the arena. Maureen was sitting on the ground, staring daggers at Hero. He was standing quietly about ten feet away with a guilty expression, reins dangling in the dirt. "What happened?" I yelled.

"What do you think? The bastard bucked me off!"

I stifled a laugh and offered a nonsensical comment. "I'm sure he didn't mean to."

"What the hell are you talking about?" she screamed. "The son of a bitch threw me. No horse throws Maureen Farrell!"

So the spoiled brat had a foul mouth! "Are you all right?" I asked, offering a hand.

She nodded. "I think so."

I helped her to her feet. She stretched, rubbed her back and dusted off her seat. Then she confronted Hero, nose to nose. "Don't ever do that again, mister!" He didn't so much as blink. They glared at each other for the longest moment.

Finally, I asked, "Do you want to try again?"

She removed her helmet and shook out her hair. "Give me a minute."

"Would you like to hear an off-the-wall suggestion?" I asked, expecting her to reject help of any kind.

She glared. "This better be good!"

"I think he's suffering from post-Selina stress syndrome."

"Really! That's a new one! How do you fix it?" she

growled.

I explained that the boarders at Trails End Stables had claimed that Hero and I immediately hit it off after Selina died because he had seen us together so often, even behaving affectionately in his stall. Hero recognized us as his support group, and he trusted us, separately or together. But he hadn't made that connection with Maureen, yet. She was a stranger. She needed to show him that the three of us were a team.

"That's ridiculous! Horses are not that sensitive! Are you suggesting the three of us have to sleep together before I'm accepted?" That triggered an amusing picture, but I dared not laugh.

I lowered my head to hide a grin. "No, but I'd like to try something, if you're game."

"I don't believe this! All right, what?" she asked, the corners of her mouth turning down in disgust.

I placed my arm around her waist and pulled her close, directly in front of Hero. "Remember – affection is the key," I said. "Now, put one arm around my back. That's it. Come on – smile. Stroke his head and jaw with me – okay, now give him some sweet talk."

"Beautiful baby," she softly said, over and over, rubbing his face.

"That's good."

Looking Hero in the eye, I added, "This is our new friend, Maureen. She's a good person, and she's now part of the team."

I squeezed Maureen and said, "Keep petting him and talking....and, for God's sake, smile!"

She elbowed me in the ribs. "I'm trying! I'm trying!" she said, kissing me on the cheek to confirm our attachment.

"Okay, now together, let's walk around him," I said.

As Maureen and I circled Hero, arms wrapped around each other, rubbing his back and sweet talking, I could feel his body soften. Maybe the treatment was working. I'd have to patent this thing.

When we stood in front of him again, I continued to whisper encouragement and to hold Maureen close. She turned and planted a hard, prolonged kiss on my parted lips. I was caught off guard, but what a good kisser! Even though Hero's a gelding, I was sure he sensed how positively I'd responded.

"That ought to do it," I said, wiping my mouth. "Would you like to try him again?"

"After all that, I guess I'll have to," she said.

She snapped her chin strap, climbed aboard, grabbed the reins, leaned along his neck and murmured in his ear. "Hero, I love you, but you only have one more chance. If we don't make it this time, it's *adios, amigo*." Then, with a pat on his shoulder and a squeeze of her leg, she urged him to walk. "Good boy!"

After a few trips around the arena, walking at first, then trotting, she halted in front of me. "Now, do me a favor. Disappear for five minutes. That will be the real test.

If he throws me, we're through here."

I climbed over the fence, jogged back to the stable and peeked out a narrow window. Maureen posed motionless, waiting for Hero to stop watching for me. Finally, he turned back and focused on the course. There was no sign of discontent or resistance.

Maureen gritted her teeth and nudged him forward. So far, so good. Next, she had him trotting – circling the arena and the jumps to get acquainted with what was expected of him. When they paused to rest, I returned.

Leaning on the fence, I said, "Mission accomplished! You guys look great together! Maybe some fate here, after all."

She smiled, pleased with the change in Hero. "Simon, I'm not good at compliments, but you might be a genius. I kid you not."

"I think it was the kiss that did it!" I said.

She laughed. "Maybe so."

I was relieved. Things were improving between us.

Abruptly, Maureen's expression went from sweet to stern. "Simon, I'm going to canter him awhile. If you would lower those far jumps to about two-and-a-half feet, I'll start him out there."

"At your service." I scrambled into the arena. I'd gone from lover to lackey in the swish of horse's tail.

26

As I set the rails, Maureen kicked Hero into a brisk canter. They circled the arena then began weaving around the jumps, alerting Hero that the exercise was underway. He'd had such a long layoff, I was uneasy about his strength and timing.

Maureen guided him to the single jump which he stumbled over. Crossing the double, he appeared lethargic and knocked off both top bars.

I replaced the rails, and she started again. The result was the same.

A horse that discontinues its training routine, even for a few months, may require a series of graduated drills to bring him back. But I knew Hero, and he was no ordinary horse.

When she halted in front of me, I asked, "Can I make a suggestion?"

She pouted like a spoiled brat. "I'm sure he's just out of shape, but what brilliant idea do you have in mind this time?"

She obviously didn't want advice from me – or maybe from any man. But I plunged ahead. "When Selina started Hero in practice sessions," I said, "she'd do flat work for twenty minutes and work him through a winding Callavetti course for another fifteen or so, then begin jumping – but never under three feet. She'd discovered that anything lower never got his attention and seemed counterproductive."

Maureen shook her head. "That's not my way and not what George Morris teaches. I start my horses out low." Frowning, she paused, bowing her head. Finally, she looked up and declared, "Oh, all right, set them at three foot three!"

From the first jump, Hero's body language revved up. His eyes widened, ears pricked up and his tale swished. This was the champion I'd seen Selina train.

Game on. Maureen sat erect, heels down, her well-rounded seat nestling into the saddle. Reluctantly, I had to admit horse and rider made a striking team, like they'd worked together for months.

I gradually adjusted the jumps 'til they reached four feet. The higher I set them, the more talented horse and rider looked.

At last, Maureen pulled up. "Simon, let's stop there. That's more than enough. This guy's special, no doubt about it. As much as I hate to admit it, you're full of bright ideas."

Hero, breathing heavily, nudged my chest with his flared nose. He obviously loved being back at work. This creature was born to compete, not become a weekend trail horse or grow old and lazy in a pasture.

"You two could clear a seven foot Puissance," I joked.

She managed a wry grin. "It wouldn't take much to get him there."

She glanced at her watch. "It's too late for our trail ride. Let's put him up and head home."

We hosed and rubbed down Hero, gave both horses carrots, checked their water and said goodnight. The sun was beginning to set as we strolled up the hill to the house.

Maureen rested her hand on my shoulder. "Simon, thanks. You made my day. I was ready to call it quits – twice."

Flattery would not come easy to this gal.

"You're welcome," I said. "But I had the advantage of knowing Hero's quirks. After a week or two, you'd learn how to make him a winner again."

She hooked her arm around mine. "Whatever....you came up with that crazy lovefest that kicked it off. And I never would have started him at over three feet – that's not by anyone's book. Now, we need to talk about this treasure of an animal." As we neared the house, she added, "Let's have a beer on the stoop and discuss where we go from here."

I removed the house key from the flower pot and returned with two Millers and a plate of saltines and

Velveeta slices. We sat on the squeaky steps and admired the Oklahoma sunset. The sky was a soft, cloudless blue and the sun's orange rim blended to a red center. I could feel the heat, but in fifteen minutes, it would be down, and we'd need jackets.

As I struggled to twist the top off her beer, I threw her a curve ball that she needed to field before we could move on. "Maureen, before we discuss Hero, I'd like to get your take on something I've heard."

There was the trace of a scowl. "What is it?" Her words had an edge. This was probably the real Maureen – my way or the highway.

"A year ago, a family from Philadelphia bought two Irish horses – just as you did – which were also stolen. My information is that the purchasers never pressed for an investigation and settled for the insurance money. Do you know anything about that?"

"I do. Dad talked to them, and you're right, that was their decision. Their name's Cranfield. Met the entire family at the Devon show last summer."

"Is it possible the Cranfields fabricated the theft, resold the horses and collected the insurance money?"

She shook her head. "The Cranfields are Main Line, elite Philadelphians, but down-to-earth horse people. True horse lovers don't manipulate the business. They do the honorable thing." Maureen took a deep breath then exhaled fire. "And if you have it in the back of your head that my father and I might be capable of such a hoax, you and I are through, and you can walk home!"

I was momentarily speechless. "Oh no, not at all" I said. "I was just wondering if you knew anything about the Cranfields. You cleared that up."

She jumped up. "Okay. I'll get us another beer, and we can discuss Hero's future. It might take a while."

"Good idea." Phew! I had to ask that, but for a minute, I thought I'd sunk the ship.

When she returned, she slid closer and rested her hand on my shoulder. I was reminded of my version of an old adage: *Beware of a gorgeous woman offering a free horse or seeking favors.*

At length, Maureen outlined an arrangement whereby she would take over the training and competitive career of Hero. She would be responsible for all expenses, including the substantial show fees, and we would split her winnings and any other compensation.

"That doesn't seem fair to you. What's the catch?" I asked.

"Well, I'll be honest. I live to compete, and at the moment, I don't have a decent horse to show, just a few young ones in training. That's why we bought those two from Ireland.

"Hero's a talented horse and ready to go. Even if I were lucky, it would take months, maybe a year, to bring my best one up to his level. So a horse that's ready to go is worth a great deal to me."

"I get it." I grinned. "But let's be honest – Hero's not

just a *talented* horse, he's already Olympic caliber. Your horses aren't even close to Grand Prix – maybe not for years. So how about throwing in a couple of thousand to sweeten this deal?"

Maureen laughed. "Okay, mister, you've got my number! So let's try another approach." With that, she suddenly threw her arms around my neck and began kissing me. First on my cheek, then long and hard on the mouth with that luscious, full mouth. She formed her body to mine and pressed hard, bone on bone.

I recognized an invitation to dance, and I knew the steps. Besides, she'd been a tease and needed to be taught a lesson. I backed her against the stairs and fiercely returned her kiss. She opened her mouth, and we were off to the races.

She tore at my shirt and groped for parts of me that weren't accustomed to such unladylike handling. Breathing heavily in my ear, she whispered, "If we have a deal, we should seal it upstairs."

With one hand squeezing her supple bottom and the other fumbling with her bra, how could I stop and discuss business? "Okay – you're on," I panted. This contract needed to be consummated in a hurry.

We staggered through the door and up the staircase – groping and kissing while banging back and forth against the walls. This gal played rough.

There was a dimly lit bedroom off the landing. We stumbled in, and she pushed me down on a narrow bed and jumped on top, tearing off her blouse and wrestling with my belt.

"Do you have any protection?" she shrieked.

I hesitated. "No! I didn't plan this!" It was her party – let her deal with security.

"Sure enough," she said, "I'll take care of it ...."

No need to worry about her bra – she ripped it off, releasing her lusty breasts! Then she stripped me down, grabbed my third member and wiggled underneath me. "Give it to me hard!" she shouted.

I guess new experiences are the spice of life, but this was like an entire meal of chili peppers.

What followed was more than frantic – it was violent. With our bodies arching and thrashing, the narrow bed rattled and bounced us into the air. On a final flight of ecstasy, we shared a screaming explosion and hit the floor with a thud.

"Out of this world!" Maureen shouted.

I lay on my back, dazed and panting. As my eyes adjusted to the darkness, I scanned the ceiling and walls. There was something familiar about this room. Then my heart plunged. "Oh no! God, no!"

"What's wrong?" Maureen demanded, still groaning and spread eagle on the floor.

Words stuck in my throat. There was a faint odor of *Dolce & Gabbana Light Blue* – her favorite perfume. And I couldn't believe who'd been watching us. P. J. and Transport, her beloved horse that had been bitten by the snake, and P.J. with a gardenia in her hair, being escorted by a tuxedoed prom date – and others. They were all eyeing us through framed glass from above the bed and the bedside table.

This was P. J.'s room – the inner sanctum where she'd grown from little girl to beautiful young woman.

Stunned with guilt, I struggled to my knees, shaking my head. *What kind of person was I? On second thought, maybe just a normal man.*

27

BEFORE THE KNACKERMAN ARRIVED AT ST. CLERANS TO HAUL OFF CLANCY'S BODY, GRADY QUINN WHISKED ME AWAY IN A BLACK LAND ROVER. He'd persuaded me to bottle my grief and proceed with the plan to check the flight records at Shannon Airport.

The newly appointed equine inspector, Bryan Fahey, was expecting us in an hour. If I were driving on these narrow roads, it would take twice that, even without a livestock blockade.

It wasn't raining, but the sky was dark and heavy – like my heart. I loved Clancy. We hit it off from the first night when he'd come knocking at my patio door. And our bond was sealed forever when he safely packed me around the sloppy Galway countryside. It took all my self-control to contain my tears. Whoever shot Clancy knew I cherished him, and they'd also learned of my anguish over Transport's thin hold on life. The culprit or culprits figured

I'd be so distraught, I'd throw in the towel and leave Ireland immediately. But they'd never dealt with an Oklahoma City police officer. And they probably didn't realize I'd found an Irish protector in Grady Quinn – a fearless man with the strength of a bear.

Once we'd headed south on the N18, I said, "I'd like to call my father and check on Transport. He should be recovering from surgery."

Grady nodded. "P.J., you don't need my permission."

On the third ring, Dad answered. "How's Transport doing?" I asked.

"Parker, I'm glad you called. Dr. Jett performed the skin graft. It went well, but Transport refuses to put weight on that leg. He's spooked by those unfamiliar sensations around the ankle – suture chafing, muscle degeneration and general soreness."

"He needs to start walking, doesn't he, Dad?"

"Without walking to stimulate circulation, the tendon tissue in the lower leg will atrophy, and his career, even his life, could be over. So he's far from out of the woods, Parker."

I shook my head. My father never pulled punches, and for this, I was grateful. "I wish I were there, Dad. I'm sorry you have to deal with that alone."

"I'm fine," he said, though I could detect the strain in his voice, "and at the moment, there's nothing you can do. Maybe pray. I'll keep you informed."

He paused, then asked, "Have you discussed things

with Simon? He came to the farm with Maureen Farrell to take a look at Hero. I had an emergency at Vet Med and had to rush off. Never really had time to talk to him."

"What? He brought her to the house?" I paused to calm myself. "We haven't talked – I need to call him," I said, controlling my irritation, then said goodbye.

I decided not to burden my father with Clancy's murder. He had enough on his plate.

But now I had another worry. Why hadn't Simon called me and said he was squiring that woman around my home?

Grady touched my shoulder. "Everything all right?"

"Not really. My horse in the U.S. is still critical. And I need to contact Simon."

He smiled. "I won't listen."

I punched his arm. "You're a good man."

Twenty-four hours earlier, I'd mistrusted Grady Quinn. But his concern for me during the foxhunt, and his apparent desire to assist in the investigation indicated he probably wasn't involved in the horse theft. Of course, his macho appeal could be deceiving – wouldn't be the first time.

When I phoned, Simon was packing a bag for his flight to New York. Maureen had pulled some strings, and they were off to examine the equine records at Kennedy International.

I quizzed him about his visit to Chandler. He claimed he'd been on a fast track. Miss Farrell had pressured him to allow her to evaluate Hero in exchange for a free airlift to the Big Apple. That made sense, but he sounded uncomfortable, maybe gulity. With Quinn next to me, I decided not to ask any more questions and said goodbye.

"Is himself behaving?" Grady asked with a chuckle.

I was upset but managed a feeble smile. "Everything's fine. Simon's on his way to Kennedy. After Shannon, he and I will compare notes."

Worried sick about Transport and confused over Simon, I stared out the window. For most of the drive from St. Clerans to Shannon Airport, Grady accepted my glum silence.

When the sun popped through the scattering clouds, spotlighting the cottages and diminutive farms, I took in the verdant beauty of Ireland. Still I missed home. And if I wanted a relationship with Simon Rush, I ought to be there. If he was straying, he wasn't entirely to blame. I'd pushed him away when we were about to leave England, encouraging him to resolve his feelings for Emma Fergusson-Sloan. Still, I thought Simon and I had reached an understanding. But something may have gone wrong.

The equine loading hangar at Shannon was on the far side of the main terminal. Attached to the hangar was a metal canopy, covering ten to twelve portable stalls. Several horses were munching hay, while others gawked over their gates, trying to figure out why Grady and I were there.

Six two-horse and three four-horse aluminum flight containers were parked in front. One of the two-horse crates was being loaded.

Grady and I stopped to observe the boarding process. Three men were involved. The groom that would be traveling with the horses handled the doors, the second led each horse up the ramp into the transport and the last one, swishing a whip, stood behind the animal to make sure it kept moving into the shadowy container.

They were having trouble with a big, agitated gray that refused to enter. While the man leading the horse jerked on his halter and the worker in the rear swirled his whip and tapped his butt, the panic stricken horse tried to leap off the ramp. Then in a flash, it took two steps back and kicked, catching the man handling the whip full-bore in the chest. The blow flipped him into the air like a matador off the horns of an enraged bull. He met the tarmac with a thump and lay there motionless.

Grady rushed forward and shouted, "Call an ambulance! Don't move this man 'til it comes!"

Two men flew out of the "Office" door. The smaller one, in a green plaid jacket, brought to mind the word *leprechaun*. "Medical transport's on the way!" he called.

Grady murmured to me, looking over his shoulder, "The elf is Bryan Fahey. He should have been out here supervising the loading."

We exchanged greetings with Fahey. The downed man was breathing but couldn't speak. Soon the medics arrived and loaded him in an unmarked van and sped off.

Bryan motioned us into his office. His quarters

needed refurbishing – torn lace curtains in the windows, old fashioned roll-top desk, uncomfortable folding guest chairs and rows of pitted file cabinets along the walls.

He pointed for us to sit down then shimmied onto a high back swivel chair. He'd have to scale down some furniture but was probably waiting till Doyle Crouch, his predecessor, was cold in the grave.

Bryan swept back his curly black hair and took a deep breath. "Sorry 'bout that. New man. Never should stand directly behind any horse. Ought to know better. Now, what can I do for you lovely people?"

Grady glanced at me then said, "This is P.J. Porter from the U.S. Herself has a couple of questions concerning the horses shipped to the Farrells in the U.S. But before we get into that, we'd like your opinion on the death of Doyle Crouch."

Bryan shifted in his seat. "Well, at first, it was considered an accident. Then, rumor had it, 'twas murder, but from what's been reported, there's no proof. Last I heard, Sean O'Malley was suspected. Maybe Doyle discovered a crime in progress, and O'Malley had to get rid of him. But that's more speculation."

"Could O'Malley and Crouch have been working together and had a falling out?" I asked.

Again, Fahey palmed his hair. "'Tis possible. Sean was here many times shipping horses. That might've led to a black-hearted alliance. But I lived in Cork at the time – here just one or two days a week to assist – so I'm not the best person to ask."

"How about Sergeant McConnell?" I asked. "Ever see him around here?"

Bryan shook his head. "Not atall."

I paused. "The main reason for our visit," I said, "is that last month, Sean O'Malley shipped two horses – Rock of Cashel and Resident Magistrate – to Kennedy International in New York. We'd like to see what your records show."

Bryan slid off his chair then climbed on a step stool and pulled out one of the cabinet drawers. "Let's have a look. I remember those two. They were famous."

He riffled through the records then pulled out a folder. "Here 'tis."

I couldn't help but smile at his miniature stature and thick, Irish brogue. "Were their passports and microchips checked?" I asked.

He ran his finger down the page. "Everything appears in order. And the horses left for Kennedy on schedule." Flipping to the next page, he paused and scratched his head. "Hold on – what's this?"

"What's what?" I asked.

"Another bill of lading, the same day. This is odd. The names are similar – Hard Cash and Local Judge. But look at this...."

"What is it, Bryan?" Grady demanded, getting out of his chair.

"The destination is Kennedy, but there's a line run

through it with initials to the side."

"What are the initials?" This was like pulling teeth.

"Looks like *RT/FMcB*."

Bryan's eyes darted around the ceiling as if searching for divine revelation. Finally, he said, "RT doesn't mean anything to me, but FMcB might. That person was around here at the time."

"Come on, man! Who was it?" Grady bellowed.

"Fiona McBride."

28

"Limerick is twenty minutes from here," Grady said as we climbed into his Land Rover.

He knew where Fiona's widowed mother lived. I wondered if he had ever dated Fiona. I'd ask later.

The narrow asphalt road from Shannon was lined with hedgerows and humming with small-car traffic. Grady was a master at maneuvering in Irish congestion so I relaxed.

I wondered about Doyle Crouch. He was the X-factor. He hadn't leaped off the Cliffs of Moher for a swim. The more I learned, the more complex this horse rustling thing became. What sort of person or persons murders people over a couple of horses? Besides the Farrells and the Cranfields, could there be more victims in America and abroad? Just keep digging, I thought.

"Grady, how well did you know Doyle Crouch?" I asked. "Could he have been involved in the horse theft?"

"Anything's possible. I first met him when he was

hired as the equine inspector at Shannon Airport, five years ago. We'd only see each other when I had a horse to ship. He was a quiet loner, hard to know, but serious about his commission."

"Where did he come from?" I asked.

Grady paused. "I didn't know the family, but I've heard they emigrated to the states when Doyle was a young man and returned after he'd grown. 'Tis the custom here, ya know. After a few years, some Irish abandon their success in America to return to the ol' sod."

Abruptly, with the finesse of a Daytona racer, Grady whipped around a hay truck that had been shedding dust and straw, interfering with his vision, then calmly resumed. "Doyle performed similar work in the States, either in New York or New Jersey. That's how he qualified for his position at Shannon."

Grady Quinn would be cool under fire – maybe elsewhere.

The highway fed into the heart of Limerick. I'd read that it was the republic's fourth largest city – population about 75,000. I thought there was a grimness about the place. Most of the white stucco houses had weathered to gray, and the narrow cobblestone streets had darkened with age and silt.

As we wound from the commercial district to lower-class residential, I watched scruffy children playing hopscotch and pitch-penny on the sidewalks. I wondered if Frank McCourt, the Pulitzer Prize winner, had spent his miserable childhood in this neighborhood.

Grady turned the Land Rover into a narrow alley, locked it, and we set out on foot.

For the most part, Killarney Street was dreary. Fiona's home at 822 was a row house made more inviting with its blue door and window boxes overflowing with geraniums and petunias. A small brass plate was inscribed *R. T. Mc Bride*. The initials were familiar.

Grady knocked. No answer, so he rapped again. The door opened slightly. A middle aged woman in a floral print dress peered out. She adjusted pins in her untidy hair and dabbed her red and swollen eyes with a handkerchief.

"Can I help ye?" she asked in a quivering brogue.

I stepped forward. "We're sorry to disturb you, ma'am. Are you Fiona McBride's mother?"

"Right, I'm Rose McBride. And you?"

"P.J. Porter from the United States, and this is Grady Quinn."

"I'm acquainted with himself. If you're looking for Fiona, she's not here. She recently passed, if you didn't know." She sobbed and sagged against the door frame.

Grady took her arm and escorted her into a modest parlor. "Let's sit a moment, Mrs. McBride. If you're able, we'd just like to ask a few questions, then we'll leave you to yourself."

The room appeared freshly painted, and the settee and two lounge chairs were tastefully upholstered in solids and prints. A framed, black and white, photograph of a young woman, presumably Fiona, on a spotted horse hung over the couch. In front of the sofa sat a small, painted table with a simple porcelain tea service. Yellowed lace curtains shielded the room from nosey pedestrians.

Once Rose collected herself, she insisted on putting the kettle on, then carried the tea pot into the miniature kitchen. Although it had been modernized, an antique water pump in the corner of the sink caught my eye. "It doesn't work – just reminds us how things were," she said, sighing.

We stood silent and awkward while the kettle came to a near boil. She measured three spoonfuls of tea from a tarnished tin into the pot, added hot water and carried it back to the living room with a plate of scones. Waiting a moment for the tea to brew, she poured through a dainty sieve, placing one of the hard-looking biscuits on the edge of each saucer. It was apparent that this traditional gesture of hospitality kept her busy and relieved, though briefly, her preoccupation with Fiona.

I spoke softly, assuring her that her cooperation might throw new light on her daughter's death. Smoothing her hair and then her dress, Rose apologized for her emotional state. Fiona's death had been a devastating shock. Still, she seemed to welcome the opportunity to talk.

"Fiona was ne'r a problem or burden to the family," she sighed. "The darlin' loved horses – mated and sold them since she was a wee one on the family farm."

With that she began to weep and again dabbed

her eyes with her handkerchief. "Sorry. Very sorry," she sobbed.

When she calmed down, Rose proceeded to explain that when her husband died in a tractor accident four years earlier, the homestead was sold, and mother and daughter moved to Limerick. Later, Fiona went off to Galway City to look for a job. Even then she continued to work part time with other horse dealers in locating and exporting promising show horses.

"Did Fiona ever mention Ross McConnell?" I asked.

She nodded. "Oh yes. He's from Limerick, as well. They both attended St. Catherine's primary school."

I glanced at Grady. "Could they have been in the horse business together?" I asked.

"Ah, I wouldn't know. She never spoke of that atall."

I was reluctant to upset her further, but at the same time, anxious to obtain all the information I could. "Mrs. McBride, let me ask you something else," I said. "Shannon Airport records indicated Fiona might have shipped horses to the U.S. with someone with the initials R.T. I notice those are the initials on your door. What do you make of that?"

"R.T. were my husband's initials – Robert Tyre McBride. He carried a heart the size of his head in his chest. But he's passed. Sorry, I don't know anything more.

"Would you like another cup?" she asked, reaching for the pot.

Grady looked sideways at me, and I shook my head.

"No, thank ye, Mrs. McBride," he replied. "We'll be off in a minute. Please accept our condolence for the tragic loss of both your husband and daughter."

She broke down and bawled. I moved next to her on the settee and took her hand. "You have my sympathy, Mrs. McBride. I was riding with the Blazers when Fiona had her accident."

She took a deep, shuddering breath. "As if her passing wasn't enough, the Gallway coroner had more bad news for me just today."

Grady rose and sat down on her other side. "Rose, can you share that with us?" he asked.

"It will be in the newspaper soon enough, I suppose. During the autopsy, they discovered Fiona was pregnant. Lord, she wasn't married! Not even engaged!" She dropped her head into her hands, and her entire body shook.

I placed my arm around her shoulder. "I'm so sorry. Do you have any idea who the father might be?"

"Not atall. The only man she ever mentioned was her school friend, Ross McConnell. But I never thought they were close."

Grady shot me an angry, inquiring look.

* * * * * * *

I'd been reluctant to discuss the case with Sergeant McConnell for fear of being charged and detained for interfering. That just changed. Now, I was eager to confront him. I wanted an explanation of Fiona's hunting *accident* and his take on the drowning of Doyle Crouch. Also, I'd like to challenge his accusation that Sean O'Malley had swindled the Farrells, and I might even inquire about Fiona's pregnancy.

We thanked Rose for the tea and again extended our sympathies. I asked if I could call someone to come and be with her, but she shook her head.

Grady seemed just as anxious to question McConnell as I was and offered to drive me to police headquarters in Galway City on our way back to St. Clerans. I accepted, and we sped north.

We drove without speaking, listening to the purr of the engine and weighing what Rose McBride had revealed. Finally, Grady, his brow furrowed, said, "I'm confused. Even if Fiona were romantically involved with McConnell, that wouldn't mean they were working together in the horse thefts. It could be completely irrelevant."

For the first time since leaving St. Clerans that morning, I smiled. This intelligent Irishman was more baffled than as I was.

"Well, let's speculate for a moment," I said. "The tension between Ross and Fiona during dinner at St. Clerans confirmed they'd had an off and on relationship. Whether he'd be the father of her child is something else. But an intriguing tidbit from Rose was that Fiona had kept her hand in the horse-business. And remember that the initials on the Shannon to Kennedy records were *RT/FMcB*. This seems to fit with a theory that keeps rolling around in my head."

"What's that?"

I removed my ball cap and shook out my hair. "Grady, is it possible that Ross McConnell's first two initials are R. T.?"

He thought about that for a second. As he was about to answer, the Land Rover was suddenly jarred from behind by another vehicle, and we served violently. While Grady struggled to keep the car under control, I looked around to face the front end of a huge lorry on our tail. "Who is that maniac?" I screamed.

The truck looked familiar, but the driver sat above my line of sight. He backed off, revved his engine and rammed us again. The Land Rover swayed and nearly spun off the road.

"Hang on, Grady!" I yelled. "There has to be a turn off or field up ahead!"

"He's trying to kill us!" Grady shouted as the lorry jolted us again and again, and he wrestled with the wheel.

When the Land Rover began to rock, it became too much. "Hold on!" Grady cried out as we smashed through a wooden barricade, spinning toward a watery ditch at the bottom of the embankment. We rolled over and over, glass splintering and our bodies crashing against the doors and the roof and the dashboard like tennis shoes in a clothes dryer.

With blood gushing from my nose, I screamed, "God, help us!"

At the final second, Grady released the wheel and threw his arms around me. "I've got ya, dear!" he wailed.

The last thing I remember was the bone-crunching impact when we hit the bottom.

29

I'D FINISHED BREAKFAST ON THE FARRELL'S VERANDA AND WAS ADMIRING THE WATERFALL AND ELABORATE FLORA WHEN MAUREEN JOINED ME. She had a gleam in her eye which implied that after yesterday, we were no longer just business partners.

"Good morning, lover boy. You ready to go?" she asked with a chuckle.

Oh, God! What would P.J. say if she were here? Probably knock both of us on our butts.

I smiled, making my best effort to be congenial. "Let me grab a jacket, and I'll meet you at the plane."

It took some restraint not to complement her on how smart she looked in her powder blue jet suit.

The flight to New York City was easy compared to locating the equine import facility. We landed at LaGuardia, caught a taxi to Kennedy International, from there took a shuttle to the animal holding center and went through security for the second time that day. Once there, Maureen began throwing her weight around. Within moments we were assigned a uniformed officer, Inspector Konrad Kobe, "to assist Miss Farrell from Dallas." He wasn't pleased about being pulled off whatever he was doing, but Maureen's charm quickly smoothed his ruffled feathers.

The equine facility was an oversized barn – twenty-five percent devoted to paper work and the balance divided into two sections, each containing approximately fifty stalls. We were informed that one set of stalls was for horses detained because of suspected health issues, and the other for those being expedited to the New York Animal Import Center (NYAIC).

Any horse obviously infected with a contagious disease not common in the U. S. was immediately flown back to where it had come from. Other questionable animals were quarantined until their blood samples could be analyzed.

The majority, however, were processed by having their passports and microchips checked, blood samples drawn and the animals shipped by land transport to NYAIC for thorough medical examinations.

I explained to Mr. Kobe, a tall, thin, balding man, wearing Coke-bottle thick glasses, that we were attempting to confirm the arrival of two or four show jumpers from Shannon Airport a month earlier. He sat down at a computer and began typing.

"Here it is," he said, pointing. "There were two containers that left Shannon the same week – one transporting Resident Magistrate and Rock of Cashel – the other, Local Judge and Hard Cash." He punched some more keys. "Hold on!"

"What's the matter?" I asked.

"Local Judge and Hard Cash never made it. They appear to have been rerouted from Ireland directly to RT – that's Rock Tavern where the NYAIC is located."

"What do you mean 'rerouted?'" I asked.

"Well, most of the horses that arrive at Kennedy from overseas are transferred to NYAIC for medical tests. However, a handful of renowned animals, participating in imminent competitions, are allowed to be flown straightaway to the RT."

Maureen interrupted. "What are they tested for?"

"Primarily Piroplasmosis, Douring, Glanders, Equine Infectious Anemia, West Nile and African Horse Sickness – diseases that are relatively rare in this country, but could cause an equine epidemic.

"These sicknesses are uncommon in Ireland, but we catch some that pass through, coming from other countries. It's a tricky business."

"You mentioned that some horses can bypass Kennedy. How does that work? Do they avoid the medical examinations, too?" I asked.

"Not at all," he replied, shaking his head. "Those horses are pre-tested at the point of departure. The U.S.

accepts such foreign screenings, subject to us having good relations with the exporting country. For example, we recently fast-tracked Last Hurrah, the famous English eventer, participating in the Rolex Three Day in Kentucky."

"I've never heard of that. Does the Import Center have an adequate airport?" I asked

"One of the largest commercial strips in the country. But it takes political stroke to land there."

"Could we see the NYAIC? How far away is it?" I asked.

Mr. Kobe frowned and removed his glasses. "Ninety miles up the Hudson River, but I'd have to clear it with Dr. Dante Helm, the Director. I warn you, though, he dislikes visitors. He'll claim he's too busy."

Maureen produced her captivating smile. "Konrad, it's important. We're trying to find a horse thief who also kills people. Wouldn't you please try?"

What would I do without her?

Kobe scratched his head. "Tell you what I'll do, Miss Farrell. I'll call Dr. Helm and introduce you, and you take it from there. Maybe you can persuade him."

Maureen glanced at me. I nodded. "Get him on the phone," she said.

Kobe dialed away. When someone answered, he said, "This is Konrad Kobe calling from Kennedy International. May I speak to Dr. Helm?"

After listening to the reply, Kobe turned to us. "He's in one of the barns. They want me to leave a number. He'll call back."

Maureen shook her head.

"Let me talk," I said.

He handed me the phone. "This is Simon Rush. I'm with Maureen Farrell from Dallas, Texas. She shipped two horses from Ireland that were stolen somewhere between Shannon Airport and your facility. It's urgent that we speak to Dr. Helm before turning this matter over to the NYPD."

The woman at the other end said, "Just a minute."

I waited for what seemed like five. "This is Dr. Helm," a man said in a stern, German voice. "What can I do for you?"

"Dr. Helm, I'm Simon Rush. Miss Farrell and I would like to talk to you in person. Just for a few minutes. We're trying to locate two valuable horses that were heisted. We could rent a car and be there in three hours."

I could hear him inhale. "What's your name again?"

"Simon Rush."

"Mr. Rush, we're overwhelmed here, but I'll give you ten minutes, no more! And I mean it!"

"Good enough. We're on our way," I said and hung up. This doctor had the phone etiquette of a bill collector.

After several wrong turns and a stop for directions, we swung onto the Hudson River Parkway and headed north. Maureen turned off the car radio. "Why didn't the NYPD check the Kennedy import records when the horses were stolen?" she asked. "They could have done just what we did in half the time."

I nodded. "You're right! In fairness though, the investigation from the start was centered in Ireland. Everyone believed the stolen animals were either hidden in Ireland or shipped from there to Europe. P.J. stumbled onto this other possibility only yesterday."

Maureen shook her head. "Still, it doesn't seem like the NYPD were very thorough. Remind me to make a few calls when we return. Someone up the ladder ought to be informed," she said, tuning in a soft jazz station.

I'd never driven along the tree-lined Hudson River. It was much wider and swifter than I'd imagined – maybe over a mile across in places. It moved along as though heavy rains had filled it to capacity, and the banks were squeezing it toward the ocean.

We watched a mahogany decked yacht, possibly of Commodore Vanderbilt vintage, struggling against the current. The natty skipper, wearing traditional captain's cap, blue blazer and white flannels, waved to us enthusiastically. I rolled down the window and gave him a vigorous reply.

But the most memorable was passing the majestic U.S. Military Academy at West Point that sat high and proud on the far side of the river. From our vantage, it appeared larger than life, maybe half a mile long, with the stars and stripes flapping above ramparts reminiscent of an English fortress.

Maureen and I sat shoulder to shoulder the entire trip, but she never mentioned our assignation of the night before. Her only comment was to confirm that we still had an agreement concerning Hero to which I nodded.

NYAIC was a federal agency under the U. S. Department of Agriculture. It consisted of an office complex and seven barns, all constructed of bland, beige-colored aluminum and surrounded by an eight-foot high, chain-link fence.

An armed guard stood at the entrance. Two ominous, prancing and barking Doberman Pincers with tiger-size fangs were chained to a heavy metal stake. The place reminded me of a concentration camp.

"We're here to see Dr. Helm," I announced. "I'm Simon Rush, and this is Miss Farrell."

"Just a minute," he said, pulling a phone out of a black box. After exchanging a few words with someone, he opened the gate and motioned us to enter. "Dr. Helm says you have ten minutes. He's in his office – across the way."

Helm greeted us as if our time was already up. He was a short, stocky man with piercing dark eyes, crew cut and jutting jaw. He waved his hand at two hard back chairs in front of his desk. "Now, what is it you want?" he asked in that thick German accent.

Again, we introduced ourselves.

Helm nodded without changing his bull-dog expression.

When I attempted to review the disappearance of Maureen's horses, he punched his index finger on the desk, eager to interrupt. "Mr. Rush, it sounds like you're accusing me and the New York Animal Import Center of criminal double-dealing!"

"I'm just trying to find my horses, Dr. Helm!" Maureen demanded.

Good for her, I thought.

Helm sat back. "My assistant, Dr. Case, reviewed our files. Resident Magistrate and Rock of Cashel passed through here and were released to the Farrells' transport agent. We have absolutely no record of Local Judge or Hard Cash, or any other horses arriving directly from Shannon around that time. I suggest you look elsewhere. Now – your ten minutes are up!"

This man needed charm school. "Dr. Helm, we thank you for your time," I said, stifling my temper. "We've come a long way, sir. Is there any chance someone could show us around this impressive complex before we start back?"

Dr. Helm scowled. "Mr. Rush, this is a secured, government facility, not a tourist stop….but, I'll see if Dr. Case can spare a few minutes to point out what we do here." With that we were escorted to a spartan waiting room.

Maureen and I sat stunned and silent on a hard bench, like school children who'd just been berated by the principal. We couldn't force the hand of the U.S. government. Was this the dead end of our search?

Dr. Helm's assistant was nothing like the boss. He was tall and good-looking with long bleached blond hair and a broad, toothy smile. What a pleasant change!

"I'm Dr. Marsten Case. I understand you'd like an inspection of the facilities."

From his hand motions and voice inflections, I realized that Dr. Case could be, as my father used to say, *a little light in his loafers.*

Maureen must have recognized that she was best suited to deal with him. "Marsten. May I call you Marsten?" she cooed in a charming drawl.

"Please do."

"Marsten, by now you know what's happened. Simon and I have come all the way from New York City, and we're curious about this renowned facility. Would it be possible to see any of the barns?"

Dr. Case paused. "Sorry, that's not permitted. But I could show you the disinfectant house, if you'd like." He giggled.

"What's that?" I asked.

"Every horse that comes through here is first chemically hosed down then led through a medicated wading pool to remove any harmful bacteria. So I can't let you actually walk inside, unless you'd agree to take the same bath. Heh! Heh!" His toothy laugh made me uncomfortable.

Maureen managed a playful laugh. "We'll pass on that, Marsten."

As we strolled toward the "bath house," which was the first building, Maureen carried on a flirtatious conversation with Dr. Case. He explained the use of the seven barns, including the furthest two which were absolutely off-limits – reserved for quarantined animals. He also reviewed, in terms designed to impress, why some horses were quarantined and others not. In brief, some were clearly infection free and released to their owners, others were suspect or needed medication and were detained.

Maureen asked, "Marsten, where did you receive your veterinary education? You sound so knowledgeable."

This gal could have a future in politics.

His faced lit up. "My father was in the diplomatic service so we moved about. I finished my studies at Trinity College in Dublin."

That jolted me. A Gestapo agent and a gay horse doctor with an Irish connection! Weird! What had we stumbled into?

30

Once Maureen and I settled into the privacy of our car, she looked at me with a bewildered expression. "Can you believe those two? They operate that place like a personal business, hidden in this remote area, beyond government oversight," she said.

I nodded. "I wouldn't trust either one of them, particularly the Hun. That guy's a tyrant. And the other one gives me the willies.

"I wish we'd been able to look in those other barns. I don't understand all the secrecy." Pausing to collect my thoughts, I added, "Do you suppose we could slip in there after dark?"

Maureen threw back her head. "Are you serious? Did you see those dogs and the size of that fence? That's crazy! Besides, everything has to be locked up tight."

I chuckled. "In college, I high jumped bigger sorority fences than that. And the doors may be locked, but those barns have windows. As brilliant as you are, can't you figure out how to distract those man-eaters?"

"Ha! Maybe I can," she said, nudging my shoulder. "Just find me some ground beef to go with the Ambien I have in my bag."

In the nearby village of Rock Tavern, we bought ground beef, a flashlight and a collapsible ladder, then found a diner where we could have coffee, a bite to eat and wait 'til dark.

Washington's Larder was a remodeled caboose – faded blue outside, gray Masonite inside. I became nostalgic as I absorbed the ambience and watched the locals enjoying the home-cooked food. Diners were U.S. landmarks that sadly had begun to disappear.

As for landmarks, the back of the menu contained a little history. The original Rock Tavern, for which the borough was named, had been a popular meeting place prior to and during the Revolutionary War. But the public house has been gone for a hundred years. During the war, an encampment had been established in the vicinity, including a military hospital, which tented 6000 to 8000 troops and their families. The town's proudest moment had come when General George Washington instituted the Badge of Merit here which, over time, became the Purple Heart.

We ordered two of the "House Specials." Maureen chose meatloaf with mashed potatoes and succotash while I selected the open faced turkey sandwich with home fries, smothered in gravy. Being from Oklahoma, this was my kind of food – loaded with wholesome calories like Mother used to serve.

I was cautiously excited about our evening adventure. "I didn't see a burglar alarm," I said. "No signs or stickers on the fence and no relay boxes."

Maureen nodded as she swallowed. "Mexican cooks can't make meatloaf like this." Then she asked, "Why bother with an alarm system anyway? What's there to steal? No one wants a sick horse out of quarantine. Just lock everything up and turn loose those Dobermans. That would be security enough."

"I agree. I just hope that armed guard has a loving wife who entices him home with good food and a warm bed."

Maureen rolled her eyes. "Here! Here!"

I searched my new partner's deep blue eyes and smiled. "You're a good sport – for a spoiled, rich kid."

"I guess that's a compliment." She hesitated, then added, "It's not my fault that Far-L Ranch happened to be in the heart of the East Texas Oil Field."

I grinned. "I suppose not. But I'll bet you attract a fair number of gold diggers. It must be tough, separating the wheat from the chaff."

"There have been problems, but I've managed," she said in a more serious voice. "Make it easy for me, Simon, are you wheat or chaff?"

"Ha! Good question! Let's explore that later, over a beer," I replied, picking up the bill and standing to leave.

There were just two lamplights on the NYAIC premises, one near the front gate and one in the middle of the facility. No other cars were in the parking lot, fifty yards from the entrance.

As we crept toward the gate, there was no sign of a guard, but the dogs began to snarl and bark. Maureen had crushed eight, 10mg Ambiens into a pound of raw hamburger. I hoped that her concoction didn't send them into a Rip Van Winkle coma.

As she distracted one dog at a time with a morsel, I fed the other a potent share of the sleeping compound. Then we went back to the car and waited.

"I have a plan," I said, fingering my cell phone. "There's no need for both of us to prowl around. Let me climb over, and you stand guard. If anyone shows up, call me on the cell, and I'll come running."

"Okay, but be careful. There could still be someone hanging around, and he could be armed."

When we returned to the gate, I rattled the fence and whistled. No response. The ferocious hounds were sleeping like babies.

Using the stepladder, I climbed to the top of the fence and jumped down on the other side. Maureen pushed the ladder over the top, and I positioned it against the fence for a quick return to safety. Then I looked around. The pole lights barely allowed me to survey the facilities. No sign of a guard – yet.

Maureen slid the flashlight through the fence. "Is

your cell phone on?" she asked.

I checked and nodded. She gave me a worried look and blew me a kiss.

I responded with, "Piece of cake," and tiptoed into the shadows.

I passed the *bath house and* stopped at the second barn. The entrance was padlocked. With the help of the flashlight, I peered through a side window. The first thing I confirmed was that no guard or groom appeared to be lurking inside. Although the building was full of stalls, I could see that only half contained horses. And if I was right, they weren't horses but assorted ponies – palomino and chestnut Shetlands, six dapple-gray Connemaras and four or five sturdy black Fells with black and white feathered hooves.

I continued down the line of buildings without seeing anything unusual. When I squinted into the first quarantine barn, I was surprised to see that just one or two horses were stalled toward the rear. That seemed odd since Dr. Case implied that those barns were nearly full. As I pressed the flashlight against the window, I discovered that it was unlocked. I pulled myself up and dropped inside. No guards in here, or they would have run me off by now. As I crept toward the horses, my light darting around, I was startled by the ring of my cell phone.

"What's the problem?" I asked in a panic. "What? Who's this? Galway City Hospital! What's wrong? Oh, no! Is she alive?"

I glanced at the horses in the shadows, made a double take when something registered, spun around, vaulted through the window and ran wildly toward the gate.

31

As I raced toward the entrance, I swung my flashlight around, searching for obstacles, in particular the Dobermans that I prayed were still asleep. Then I spotted two fiery red dots that grew larger and more piercing as the distance between us closed. One of the Dobermans, rising five yards in front of me, peeled back his lips, bared his teeth and snarled and bayed like the hound from hell. Instinct and my football training kicked in. While I spotted the light directly in the dog's eyes, I feinted left, then darted right. I prayed the Ambien had at least slowed his reflexes. But as I accelerated around him, I tripped over something, falling hard on my hands and knees. Had I stumbled on the other Doberman? I expected to feel his teeth tearing at my neck or leg. Strength and stark fear propelled me to bounce up, regain my balance and take ten more of the fastest strides in my life. Never looking back, I scampered up the stepladder, balanced myself on top of the fence, hoisted the ladder up and over, then jumped down. Panting as though

I'd run a marathon, I checked my limbs and clothes – no tears, no wounds, just scraped hands. Everything was otherwise intact.

Maureen rushed up. "What happened?" she whispered fiercely in the dark. "Did you see a guard?"

I waived toward the car. "Let's get out of here!" I shouted. "I have to get to the airport. I'll tell you on the way."

Once we were headed south, I explained that I'd received a shocking call from Galway City. P.J. had been involved in an automobile accident. Police had found my phone number in her personal effects.

"Is she okay?" Maureen pleaded.

"She's alive but unconscious. That's all they'd tell me. Maureen, I'm sorry to leave you in the lurch, but I've got to catch a plane to Shannon."

She leaned against me and squeezed my arm. "I'm so sorry, Simon."

"If you'd drop me at Kennedy, I'll go standby on Aer Lingus. There's bound to be a single on one of their Shannon flights."

She shook her head. "Simon, that might take days. I have a better idea .... Josh and I can jet you there."

"Can the Gulfstream make it without refueling? And even if it could, don't you need some sleep?"

Maureen laughed. "That's no stretch for our plane – it's only a six hour flight. And Josh is always ready to go. He does nothing but sleep on his down time. As for me –

You know I'm always ready," she said, elbowing me in the ribs.

"Maureen, you don't have to do this, but I'd be indebted," I said.

She gave me one of those devastating smiles. "That's what I'm counting on, handsome."

With that she called her pilot, and instructed him to file a flight plan, gas up and be ready to go in two hours. It was just that simple. But I did have a twinge of concern. Maureen wasn't kidding – she would expect something from me that I might regret.

* * * * * * *

We took off at dusk. The New York skyline was breath-taking. The flickering lights from the offices and bridges reflected off the Hudson and created the famous thousand points of light.

When we leveled off, Maureen called her father to explain what was going on. From the muffled argument coming from the phone, he was less than pleased.

"Dad, we have plenty of fuel, don't worry.....Yes, I have my passport.....No, I don't intend to interfere with the Irish police – though they could use some prodding.....No, I'm not coming home.....I'm the major owner of this plane, and I intend to find my horses! Dad, relax. I'll be in touch." With that, she switched him off.

"Everything okay?" I asked, knowing full well it wasn't.

"He doesn't want me in Ireland – thinks I'll get in the way of the investigation – pleaded for me to turn around. You'd think he'd want me to become involved. I don't get it. For a change, maybe he's playing concerned father.

I didn't understand either. In Tex's eyes, it appeared Maureen could do no wrong. And he thrived on her larger-than-life escapades. It had to be worry over his oil wells – production must be down a few barrels.

Then I called Dr. Porter to inform him what had happened to P.J. He'd just heard from the hospital and was in an emotional state, wrestling with what to do next. I suggested that he sit tight 'til I had a chance to talk to the doctors. I'd call him as soon as we'd met with the hospital staff. He accepted that.

The night ride at 20,000 feet over the Atlantic was smooth as silk. Maureen looked back from the copilot's chair. "How 'bout some coffee or tea?"

"Black coffee sounds good."

She fixed two cups, sat down across from me and tightened her seat belt. She chuckled. "Just in case we hit one of those nasty air pockets, again."

She threw her cap on the adjacent seat, shook out her strawberry blond hair and smiled. Maureen could have been in movies. "It's been so hectic, you never told me if you saw anything in the barns at the NYAIC," she said.

I took a sip of coffee. "I ran out of time."

She nodded.

There was a lull in the conversation. Finally, I said,

"Maureen, I can't deceive you – you've been too generous. And I have so much respect for you and your father. I kept something from you because, if I hadn't, you probably wouldn't be flying me to Ireland."

Her eyes narrowed. "What do you mean?"

I unbuckled and slid across next to her. "I'm almost certain I spotted Resident Magistrate and Rock of Cashel in one of those quarantine barns. They're probably being held captive, awaiting a sale overseas."

"What are you talking about?" Her voice grew louder. "Are you saying you saw them and didn't tell me? I could have recovered my horses, and this thing would have been over! You bastard!" she screamed, and began pounding my chest with clenched fists.

"They could be sold and exported by the time we get back," she yelled, unbuckling to punch harder. "I need to call the NYPD!"

I grabbed her wrists. "Listen! The fact they're still there means the odd couple haven't found a foreign buyer, yet. And even if they have, the evaluation process and medical exams and shipping arrangements all take time. Maureen, I know there's some risk, but the thing is – P.J. and I want to solve this mess, not only find your horses but smoke out the murdering thieves. To bring the law in now might ruin everything. I've got to go to Ireland, and you have to come with me."

I dared not mention the additional reward money at stake.

I clenched her shoulders and looked deep into her eyes. "Maureen, I'm going to need your help. You're a natural at getting devious guys to talk -- you charmed that Doctor Case right out of his tassel loafers."

I could feel her relax. "Heh! You noticed that?"

"I'm going to be honest. We work well together. If you desert me, I'll be lost."

God forgive me, that was the same thing I'd told P.J.

Maureen moved in close and lifted her face. Our cheeks touched, and she sighed. I pressed my mouth against those magnificent lips. When she feigned resistance, I pressed harder. She stopped squirming. The magnetism between us was too strong. She threw her arms around my neck and kissed me back, hard. I fantasized joining the Mile High Club, but fortunately, it was a fleeting impulse.

Josh turned back to find out what was going on. "Everything okay back there?"

Maureen pulled away. "I'm not sure, but we've declared a cease fire."

"Well, figure it out," Josh called. "I'm going to need you up here, Maureen. It may get rough as we approach land, and you need to study the Shannon landing pattern. It's tricky."

"Okay, be there in a minute."

Maureen's expression had switched from irritation to desire, and now, suspicion. "You better be on the level with me and have a plan, Simon. Otherwise, Josh and I will leave you in Ireland and fly home at the drop of a shillelagh."

I nodded. "Fair enough. Just give me a chance to compare notes with P.J. After that, we might all want to throw in the towel and come home."

She grinned. "You're a regular Rasputin, aren't you?"

She paused. "All right, I'll go along. But don't overlook something that could rock your boat."

"What that's?"

"P.J. – three's a crowd. How do you plan to deal with that?"

"Maureen, I'm not sure. P.J. and I are close. Let's find the thieves, then we'll confront the personal issues."

She took my hand. "Okay....count me in."

32

The sun was peeking over the horizon when Josh and Maureen made a flawless landing at Shannon Airport.

Maureen released her pilot to fend for himself in the city, with orders to keep his cell phone charged and on. I rented a manual-shift Renault which wasn't much bigger than a golf cart, picked up a Galway City map with the major hospital circled, then found the N18 and headed north.

I was beat, probably shouldn't have been driving, but Maureen kept me alert with a *grande* coffee from the terminal and non-stop chatter. She detailed the verdant scenery and counted flocks of sheep and herds of horses grazing in the rock-lined pastures. When she ran out of landscape commentary, she asked about Hero, his quirks and strong points and his record at various venues. My knowledge of these matters was limited, but I elaborated on what I did know to keep the conversation alive.

For the moment, we sidestepped the subject of P.J.,

but I was worried. The hospital had only said she was unconscious. Was her body broken? Could she be dying? Was this truly an accident or was it an attempt on her life because of something she knew?

On the plane, I'd been devious. It was not my style, but the situation demanded it. I'd encouraged that moment of passion because I needed Maureen and her Gulfstream to jet me to Ireland and not turn around in a fit of anger. The next problem was what would happen if she became jealous, seeing any affection between P.J. and me? It would be a tightrope, juggling hurt feelings with the needs of the investigation.

Galway City Hospital was a contemporary building – four stories with rectangular tinted windows and an ultra-modern, etched-glass entrance.

Inside, the reception desk was manned by two starched, gray-haired women. "I'm Simon Rush, just arrived from the U.S.," I announced. "I'm here to check on Miss P.J. Porter, a friend from home. She was involved in an automobile accident. I was hoping to visit her and talk to her doctor."

"Miss Blake, nurse's assistant," the older one replied.

I nodded.

"Miss Porter is out of intensive care but has not been allowed visitors. Just give me a moment."

She closed a file she'd been working on and pushed back from her desk. "Since you've come a long way, Dr. McDermott might make an allowance. He's the attending physician."

I nodded. I was too tired to speak.

She motioned for us to cool our heels in the visitors' lounge then hustled down a hallway through swinging doors labeled "No Visitors."

The waiting room was furnished with Danish modern, including a round chrome and walnut table, stacked with reading materials. One wall was covered with an eye-catching mosaic seascape, labeled *Sunset on Galway Bay*. An Irish ballad that my grandmother used to sing came to mind:

> *If you ever go across the sea to Ireland*
> *Then maybe at the closing of your day*
> *You can sit and watch the moon rise over Claddagh*
> *Or watch the sun go down on Galway Bay*

I snapped back when Miss Blake returned with a tall, bespectacled man in a white coat. His mussed salt and pepper hair and puffy eyes suggested that he might be overworked, maybe been up all night.

He extended his hand. "I'm Dr. McDermott. You're here to see Miss Porter?"

"Yes, I'm Simon Rush, a friend of the family. This is Maureen Farrell, who was kind enough to fly me here."

Maureen flashed me a quirky grin, then shook McDermott's hand.

"I recently talked to P.J.'s father," I added, "and I promised to report to him on her condition. Are you her doctor?"

"I am. And I've saved you the trouble of phoning Dr. Porter. Sergeant McConnell gave me his number, and Dr. Porter and I have talked a couple of times. I gave him the particulars, and since her vitals are stable, I suggested he wait a day or so before coming over."

"Thank you. Better hearing about her condition from you than me."

"How's P.J. doing?" Maureen asked.

"Ah, 'til yesterday, she'd been in an intermittent coma. We've kept her sedated for pain. She had a close call – broken leg and one arm just above the wrist, plus concussion and contusions on her legs and back. At first, we suspected internal injuries. Fortunately, surgery was not necessary. She'll be sore, but given time, she should recover completely."

"When will she be able to leave the hospital?" I asked.

"Depends on her progress – maybe a fortnight."

"Can we talk to her?"

"Yes, but keep it brief, and one person at a time, please."

Maureen nodded.

Dr. McDermott grabbed my elbow and pulled me aside. "Mr. Rush, there's something you should know. The man she was with in the car, Grady Quinn, was killed. Battered senseless by the crash, he drowned in the ditch where their vehicle landed. I was told the Land Rover was half full of water, and he was trapped between the door and the steering wheel."

I shook my head. "Terrible! Has she been able to tell you how it happened?"

"No, but we haven't asked yet. The gardai also want to question her when she's able. 'Tis reported there were no witnesses."

"How did P.J. get out of the car?" I asked

"Sergeant McConnell believes she crawled out her sprung door and dragged herself halfway up the bank where she lost consciousness. I don't know how she managed."

"Just like P.J. – she's tough and would find a way."

Dr. McDermott adjusted his glasses. "Last night, Miss Porter was asking about Quinn, but we decided to wait 'til she was clear-headed. She thinks he's down the hall – unconscious. With you here, I believe it's time to tell her the truth. To delay would only cause further trauma. If you're up to it, we can do it together."

I hesitated.

"It's time, Mr. Rush."

Maureen found a chair and picked up a magazine, while I followed McDermott down the hall. I tiptoed into P.J.'s room. Her eyes were open, but I hardly recognized her. Her left leg, in white plaster to the hip, was suspended by a web of cord and pulleys, and her left arm, also in a cast, was supported by a bedside armrest. An IV drip was attached to her other arm. Her eyes, nose and mouth were swollen and discolored – black, blue and purple. She looked up with glazed, disbelieving eyes.

I leaned to kiss her forehead and did my best to smile. "No need to ask how you feel," I said. "You should know better than to drink Irish Whiskey and drive."

She managed a strained smile while her eyes confirmed she was pleased I was there. She tried to sit up. Dr. McDermott supported her shoulder while adjusting her pillow. At first, her words came slowly and a bit slurred. "Simon .... I'm glad you're here. How did you know?"

I pulled up a chair and stroked her hand. I explained that the hospital administrator had called me, and that Maureen Farrell had flown us here. "Are you up to talking?" I asked.

"I'm sore and doped up. But...."

McDermott edged forward and interrupted. "Miss Porter, there's a situation you must know about." He was determined to get Quinn's death out on the table. Was this the right thing to do, I wondered?

She grimaced as she tried to turn and look at the doctor.

He patted her arm and came right to the point. "I'm sorry to inform you, Miss Porter, but your friend, Grady Quinn, died in the accident."

P.J. flinched. "Oh God! That's impossible! You said he was here! Why didn't he get out?" She began to tremble and whimper. "I never got to thank him – for all he'd done for me!"

McDermott removed a small white envelop from his pocket and poured out two white pills and offered them to

P.J. with a paper cup of water. "Take this – it's Xanax, a mild sedative – will help you relax."

She swallowed the medication and wanly smiled.

My eyes moistened as I watched her suffering. Words failed me. She must have cared deeply for this Grady Quinn.

When she quieted down, Dr. McDermott added, "I'm so sorry. I knew Grady – he was a good man."

"I don't remember much. How did I get out?" P.J. asked.

"There were no witnesses," McDermott replied, "but the gardai believe you were able to crawl out. They found you unconscious on the bank."

At that moment, there was a knock on the door and the nurse looked in. "Doctor, you have a call from the Central Garda. Can you talk now?"

"I'll be right there." He reached out to shake my hand. "You and Miss Porter take a few minutes together. If you need me, I'll be on the floor for another hour."

"Thank you for taking such good care of her," I said, rising to my feet.

He signaled goodbye and slipped out.

I settled back down and took P.J.'s hand in both of mine. "You were lucky, partner. You had me worried."

An agonized grin crossed her face. "You're right – and I've thanked the Almighty."

Her eyes filled with tears. "Does Daddy know?" she whimpered.

"Both Dr. McDermott and I have talked to him. He's okay."

She caught her breath and gritted her teeth. "Good.... Now listen....at Shannon Airport, Grady and I learned that two horses, maybe the look-alikes, were rerouted from Kennedy to – an unknown destination."

I raised my hand. "P.J., we can discuss this later, when you're stronger."

Her mouth tightened. "No!" she said. "You must hear me out! Someone with the initials RT and Fiona McBride, Sergeant McConnell's old girl friend, were involved in the shipping."

She closed her eyes and leaned back against the pillow. The pills must be working. "Simon, what happened to me was no accident. I thought I recognized the truck that forced us off the road, but my mind's so foggy I can't remember where I've seen it."

A nurse peered in. "Sorry, time's up," she said. "'Doctor's orders."

"I'll be right there." I slid back my chair.

P.J. sighed. "Tell me what you've learned."

"Not now. What you told me fits with what I know. That's enough for now. You've got to rest. I'll come back tomorrow."

She pointed at me with the index finger of her good hand. "Simon, you need to confide in Sean O'Malley. It's all right. With Grady gone, he's the only one I trust. Between the two of you, you may be able to figure it out."

This was the P.J I admired – able to rise above emotional and physical anguish.

"How do I find him?"

"Talk to his cousin, Frank Reilly, at St. Clerans. Tell him I sent you."

I kissed her cheek. P.J. was a fighter. If she hadn't been fit, the crash might have killed her. And amazingly, despite the beating, she still had the tenacity to try to unravel this mess.

"Go on," she said, motioning me toward the door. "And send in Maureen."

I froze. "Why? She doesn't know anything about this. You've talked enough for today."

This is what I didn't want. Her swollen eyes narrowed even more which said *no further discussion*. "Send in Maureen – alone! I want to meet her," she said in a tired but determined voice.

33

I rose to greet Maureen as she walked down the hall, returning from her visit with P.J. From her amused expression, I suspected I'd been skewered. "You took your time," I said. "Can I ask what the two of you talked about?"

She sat down next to me. "Personal stuff."

My curiosity was mixed with panic. "Personal stuff! What's that mean?"

Maureen grinned and patted my knee. "Relax, sonny. That's confidential. But I can repeat her final requests."

"Okay, what?"

"Contact Kit Devereux immediately – give her an update. And call Dr. Mason Jett at O.S.U. for a status report on her horse, Transport.

"Also, she wants me to take care of you. That's right," she affirmed when I showed my dismay. "She's worried you may be over your head in this country. And she wants us to occupy separate rooms while we're here. I'm to have hers at St. Clerans, and you're to find your own – down the road if the manor house is full."

I nodded. What could I say?

"Let's find St. Clerans," I said, lurching to my feet. "We can discuss our next move on the way."

Nurse Blake gave us directions, cautioning us to be on the lookout for the secluded turn-off sign to the hotel.

It started to rain as we left the hospital. These narrow asphalt roads would be slick when soaked, I thought. Once we'd found the main road to Craughwell, the village near St. Clerans, Maureen asked, "Did P.J. tell you what happened to Clancy, the Irish Draft she hunted?"

"No, we ran out of time," I replied.

"He was owned by St. Clerans. P.J. thought he was a fabulous ride, but someone shot him. Vicious act! It was a warning! She wanted to remind us that the investigation has provoked some desperate criminals. Simon, I'm not sure I'm ready for all this. I agreed to fly you here, but I'm not prepared to die for your cause. And to be honest, after meeting P.J., I realize my relationship with you may be a hindrance. I don't want to interfere."

I couldn't believe she wasn't pissed.

"I understand," I said, touching her arm. "I intend to see this thing through. But I got you into this mess, and if you want to go home, you're free to leave."

She shifted in her seat. "Tell you what – I want to meet Sean O'Malley – the guy who took my money. P.J. may trust him, but I don't. After that, I'll decide what should be done."

"Fair enough." Actually, I thought it was more than fair.

The further we drove into the countryside, the heavier the rain poured. But unlike what I was accustomed to, it fell straight down, not horizontally in sheets. On the plus side, there was practically no traffic – driving on the wrong side of the road was tricky enough.

Despite the downpour, the somber landscape was soothing. The gray backdrop enabled us to relax and delude ourselves that, for the time being, all was well.

Ten minutes of silence had passed when Maureen asked, "What do you know about our contact at the hotel, Frank Reilly?"

"All I've learned is that he works at St. Clerans and is Sean O'Malley's cousin. And he's been the liaison with O'Malley, who's in hiding."

Maureen suddenly pointed. "There's the sign to the hotel! Turn! Turn!" she shouted.

I swung the wheel hard, angling down a narrow gravel road. Though it was mid-afternoon, it was nearly dark beneath the canopy of willows, oaks and pines. I switched on the headlights. Only a sprinkle of rain penetrated the dense overhang.

As we rounded a curve, my lights illuminated a tree limb stretched across the road. I braked the Renault to a skidding halt.

"I'll move that," I said, opening the door and sliding my lanky frame out of the tight bucket seat. As I grappled with the branch, dragging it toward the side of the road, I heard a pop coming from the woods and the simultaneous zing of a projectile, barely missing my head and careening off the hood of our car. I heaved the limb and dropped to my knees in the mud. Someone had taken a shot at me! What the hell was going on?

I motioned wildly at Maureen. "Get down! Get down!" Stooping over, I raced toward the car.

As I dove inside, another bullet ricocheted off the roof. "Stay low, Maureen!" I jammed the stick in gear and revved the engine, spinning the tires and spewing gravel and dirt. When we gained traction and jolted forward, a third bang shattered the rear window.

"My God! Let's get out of here!" Maureen screamed as she probed her torso for signs of a bullet wound. Fortunately, there was none.

This was hardly a case of mistaken identity. But no one except P.J. and the hospital staff knew we were in Ireland. Heh! Wait a minute! What about that call Dr. McDermott received at the hospital?

We raced toward St. Clerans, skidding round corners with pebbles flying, soaring over slick, narrow-gauge bridges, plunging through blinding puddles and screeching to a stop in front of the most aristocratic Georgian mansion I'd ever seen.

We grabbed our overnight bags, charged up the granite staircase, shoved open the double doors and, panting heavily, halted at the front desk. The clerk on duty looked us up and down, then calmly asked, "May I help you?"

Still gasping, Maureen and I looked at each other. "Someone up the road shot at us! – tried to kill us!" I stammered. "Would you call the police?"

The clerk nodded without a change of expression. "Certainly. Will you be staying with us, sir?"

I couldn't believe this guy.

Maureen stepped forward. "We're friends of Miss P.J. Porter, who has been staying here. I assume you know she was injured in an automobile accident and is in the Galway City Hospital?"

"We do, miss," he said. "We also learned that a frequent dinner guest of ours, Mr. Grady Quinn, was killed in that tragedy."

There was still no remorse about this fellow.

"Right. Miss Porter has authorized me to occupy her room for a day or so. This is Mr. Simon Rush, who'd like to stay here too, if you have *another* room. If not, maybe you can make arrangements for him somewhere else."

The attendant turned to study his reservation book. Then he announced, "Mr. Rush can occupy the Bel Air Suite for the balance of the week, if he wishes. But there is no shower – just a bathtub."

"I'd be happy with a single room," I said.

"Sorry, we have twelve suites available for our clients. There's nothing smaller."

I nodded. "What's the rate for the Bel Air?"

"Six hundred American dollars per night plus excises," he replied without a hint of apology.

I glanced at Maureen. "I can't afford that. Could you book less expensive lodging for me, maybe a bed and breakfast?"

Maureen frowned. "Simon, take the suite! We'll figure out payment later!" Then she turned toward the clerk. "Sign him up. I'll cover it with my credit card."

I registered, red-faced, and asked, "Is Frank Reilly here? We'd like to speak to him. It's important."

"Yes, sir, I believe he's in."

"We'll go to our rooms and wash up," I said. "When you reach the police, pass the call through to me. I'd like to describe the shooting. And if you can arrange it, we'd like a meeting with Mr. Reilly as soon as possible."

Upstairs, my accommodations were way beyond my needs, both in size and elegance. A closet with a shower would have sufficed. I'd have to find a way to repay Maureen, otherwise I'd be obligated even more.

The clerk connected me with the police department. "Garda Hanlon speaking. Can I be of service?"

"This is Simon Rush, an American citizen, staying at St. Clerans. Is Sergeant McConnell there?"

"Himself is not in at the moment. May I assist ye?"

I reviewed with officer Hanlon what had happened. He promised to register my complaint and have Sergeant McConnell contact me as soon as he was available. I had a fleeting suspicion that I might not hear from him.

My phone rang again. "Mr. Reilly will meet with you whenever you're ready," the desk clerk said.

"Good. Please call Miss Farrell and ask her to meet me in the lobby in fifteen minutes," I replied.

I was chomping at the bit to take a hot bath in the oversize tub but decided just to wash up and slip into some clean trousers. Maureen and I had brought only a single change of clothes, and, if we were to remain in Ireland much longer, I'd have to wash some things in the sink. She could afford the high-priced laundry service.

Maureen, out of her flight suit and into jeans, was in the reception hall when I arrived. The frowning Mr. Reilly ushered us into his office and invited us to sit. He had already heard about the shooting from the haughty desk clerk but hadn't a clue who the perpetrator might be. Since we weren't wounded, he didn't seem too concerned. Probably thought foreigners were here at their own risk, and attempted murder was the police's responsibility.

I explained to Mr. Reilly that P.J. wanted us to meet with Sean O'Malley. We figured that with his help, we might be able to wrap up the case and exonerate him.

Looking over his glasses, Reilly lowered his voice to a near whisper and said, "Well, I'll have to contact him. If O'Malley agrees, it must be after dark. Meanwhile, 'tis almost dinner time. You can eat in the main dining room or in your suites. As soon as I'm able to reach him, I call you."

"That's fine," Maureen said. "We need to stretch out."

Maureen and I agreed to dine in our respective rooms

and catch up on jet lag sleep. That would also give me the opportunity to privately talk to Kit Devereux and Dr. Jett.

The room service menu listed no prices so I suppressed my stingy nature and ordered a meal I could hardly pronounce – *Kinvara Organic Smoked Salmon with Caesar Salad & Reggiano Parmesan Cheese* followed by *Herb Roasted Loin of Lamb, Red Onion Confit & Rosemary Jus* and for dessert black coffee and *Mascarpone Sorbet with Pink Champagne*. It sounded almost too exotic to be edible. I requested that my food not be delivered for an hour to allow time for my long awaited bath.

From my room, I was able to reach Kit and gave her the highlights of what had happened in the last twenty-four hours. She was naturally upset to learn about P.J. and asked for her phone number. We agreed to talk again after I'd met with O'Malley.

Then I called Dr. Mason Jett at the Vet Med College. He had gone for the day, but his secretary assured me he'd return my call, first thing in the morning.

Finally, I drew a bath in the tub which was wide and deep enough to accommodate Henry VIII, filled it almost to the brim with steaming water, dumped in all the bath salts the hotel provided, grabbed a pamphlet from the bedside table, eased my tired, stressed frame into the glorious liquid, cleared my mind of bullets and shooters, and read:

Merv Edward Griffin, television producer, talk show host, entrepreneur (Whose estate is the current owner of

St. Clerans), *is the son of Mervyn and Rita Griffin, nee Robinson. Both his parents were Irish emigrants, Mervyn Griffin, was from County Clare, and Rita Robinson was from Tipperary. In the years following the Great Irish Famine, the population of County Clare diminished greatly because of emigration. In 1841, the population of the county was 286,000, by 1891, it had dropped to 124,000. During the famine, 50,000 people lost their lives in County Clare*

I wondered if I were destined to be one of those who never made it out of Ireland alive.

34

The phone rang as I was finishing my dinner. It was Frank Reilly, the night manager. "Mr. O'Malley will meet with you tonight," he said.

"When – and where?" I asked.

"At eight o'clock – about an hour from now – at the Huston Cottage."

He sounded tentative, like he or O'Malley or both didn't trust us.

"Where's that?" I asked.

"It's on the grounds – behind the manor house – within walking distance. When you come downstairs, I'll give you details. Will Miss Farrell be going with you?"

"Yes, she insists on meeting O'Malley."

"Fine. Come to my office at 7:45, and I'll go over O'Malley's instructions," he said.

On schedule, Maureen and I met Reilly in his office. He nervously adjusted his glasses and swept back his remaining wisps of hair. He seemed uncomfortable with acting as go-between. I wasn't exactly at ease myself, having been shot at earlier in the day.

Reilly's eyes narrowed, and he lowered his voice as if the room might be bugged. "O'Malley is worried about the gardai arresting him and restricting his ability to prove his innocence. Now he's got a bigger problem since Miss Porter and Mr. Quinn are out of the picture. Sean was counting on their help – he's made no progress on his own. But he doesn't know you – not certain whose side you're really on, so he's taking a chance."

"Well, we're not here to play Judas," I said impatiently. "Where can we find him?"

"The Huston Cottage is within the walled courtyard – on the north side of the manor. As you walk down the road you'll see the ivy-covered brick enclosure then the metal gate into the mews. The house was John Huston's retreat and his home when hunting guests filled the manor house. Except for O'Malley, no one has lived there for years.

"The front desk will give you a flashlight and rain gear. Wait for him on the entrance steps. Do not try to go inside! He's on his way!"

"Aren't there any lights?" Maureen asked.

"No," Reilly replied. "Sorry."

"This is crazy!" she said, waving her hand. "We're supposed to walk back down the road where we were shot at and enter a dark, enclosed area and wait out in the open at the mercy of anyone in the shadows with a gun! All this just to rendezvous with a stranger, who's a suspected horse thief and murderer! Simon, I don't like it!"

I nodded. "You're right – I don't like it either. But if P.J. believes O'Malley's on the level, I'm prepared to go ahead. I trust her judgment. If you'd prefer to wait here, Maureen...."

"Come on, Simon, that's not acceptable, either. I want to look O'Malley in the eye." She turned toward Reilly. "I'd like to be able to reach someone on the phone," she said, exasperated.

Reilly held up his cell. "You'll have my number, and I'll remain in the manor 'til you return."

Maureen slipped on her ball cap, pulling her hair through the back, then took a deep breath. "All right, let's go."

Wearing the borrowed rain gear and carrying our only weapon, a plastic flashlight, we stepped into the night. The rain had eased. There was a crescent moon darting among ominous clouds which added to our apprehension. We could see four or five sets of horses' eyes watching us from across the bar-ditch. If they only knew the intrigue going on within these grounds, they might not be so relaxed.

Maureen grabbed my hand. "Thank God you're here," she whispered. I switched on the light and led her around the side of the hotel, heading down the road where we were ambushed. I figured the shooter had been no more than ten or fifteen yards away when he fired. He was either a poor shot, or he only intended to scare us.

I paused and ran the beam over the path and nearby shrubs. Nothing threatening – just the gentle rustling of the trees. We found the brick wall, then the high metal gate. It was rusted and sounded like chalk on a blackboard when I tugged it open. If we were hoping to enter unnoticed, we'd just blown it. We waited a minute and listened. Not a sound – only the shrill yelp of a distant animal, probably a fox, calling for its mate.

I could see the outline of the Huston Cottage on the far side of the brick yard. I hoped for at least a dim light inside or on the porch, but nothing. We crept across the grounds to the front steps. No sign of O'Malley. I flipped off the flashlight, letting our eyes adjust to the dark. If anyone was observing us from the top of the wall, they would have a clear shot. Trying to keep a low profile, we sat down on the steps, nestled close and waited.

Five minutes passed. I was about to call it quits, when suddenly, the porch light flashed on, illuminating us. We jumped to our feet, frantically searching the top of the wall for snipers.

"Oh, God," Maureen sighed, "what now?"

Our heads jerked toward the door as it screeched open. A stocky man in Wellingtons and waxed cotton jacket peered out.

"What are you doing here?" he muttered.

Maureen squeezed my elbow. "We're supposed to meet Sean O'Malley," I said.

The man stood in the doorway for a long moment,

looking around. "I'm Sean O'Malley," he whispered as he stepped forward. "You're alone?"

"Yes," I whispered, irritated.

"You're Simon Rush and Maureen Farrell?"

I was momentarily speechless. "You scared the hell out of us, O'Malley! Yes, we're Rush and Farrell, friends of P.J. Porter."

He held the door open. "Ah, I'm sorry, but 'tis my freedom that's at stake, ya know. Come in quickly. We can talk in here."

Inside, O'Malley switched off the porch light and turned on a small table lamp. The living room resembled a Halloween spook house – windows blacked out with shades and curtains, the crystal chandelier draped with macabre spider webs, all the furniture covered with ghost-like sheets, rugs rolled up and stacked on the side leaving the floors bare and cold looking, eerie outlines on the walls where pictures once hung, and a stale odor permeating the air, confirming that the house had not been occupied for some time.

O'Malley pointed to the sofa. "Have a seat," he said, then settled back in the armchair which faced the door.

He got right to the point. "Frank Reilly told me you were shot at. I swear it wasn't me, and I have no idea who it might be." He paused, then looked at Maureen. "And before you accuse me of fraud in connection with your stolen horses, I ask that you hear me out."

We were taken back by his frankness.

He rose, went to the window and peered out, making sure there was still nothing suspicious in the courtyard. When he sat back down, I said, "So you know, P.J. brought us up to date on her investigation over here, and we've reported to her what we've learned while snooping around in the U.S. Progress is being made. But, I want to be honest with you. We're in Ireland for two reasons – to help P.J. find Maureen's stolen horses and to bring the thieves to justice. Exonerating you will be secondary. Do we understand each other?"

Sean nodded and nervously smoothed back his mass of sandy hair. It was obvious that while in hiding, he'd been unable to visit his regular hair stylist.

"For starters, give me your take on Sergeant Ross McConnell," I said. "What do you think of him?"

O'Malley shifted in his chair. "Ah, 'til the garda accused me of switching the horses, I considered McConnell a friend. But he never investigated anyone else. That made me leery, still what could I do? If I came forward, he'd lock me up. He seemed dead set on closing the case with me as the culprit. That's when I staged my suicide at the Cliffs of Moher and went into hiding. I needed time."

I paused to let that sink in. "What do you know about Fiona McBride? Could McConnell have had anything to do with her death?"

He shook his head. "Thought that was an accident. She and McConnell had an on-and-off relationship for a year or more. 'Twas told he'd partnered in some of her foals. But whether he could have caused her death, I can't say, though it seems unlikely."

"What do you mean, *partnered in her foals*?" I asked. "How does that work?"

"Ah, well, most everyone in Ireland who owns a bit of land raises horses. If not for their own riding pleasure, they're prospects for flat racing or sport horse competition. Fiona did that all her life. As I said, I'd heard McConnell had invested with her. He probably paid the stud or insemination fees to impregnate Fiona's mares, then shared in the sale of the foals. 'Tis like the lottery – people are always hoping for a champion."

That triggered another question. "Sean, according to P.J., the Shannon flight records indicated that two horses, Local Judge and Hard Cash, were shipped directly to the NYAIC at Rock Tavern, New York, and Fiona McBride's initials were on the transfers. Is it possible Fiona could have supplied the look-alike horses for the switch?"

"Well now, she certainly would have had the contacts to locate them," he replied. "There're hundreds of small breeders in Western Ireland."

Maureen rose as if to leave. "This is complicated, and it's all speculation."

I motioned her to sit back down. "There has to be a connection," I said. "What about Doyle Crouch – the shipping inspector they fished out of the drink? Could there be a link between him and Fiona, or between Crouch and Sergeant McConnell?"

O'Malley rubbed his head. "I wouldn't know about that. No one seemed to know much about Crouch, except he'd received his transport training in New York."

"Didn't he have any friends?" Maureen asked.

"No one that I knew of," O'Malley replied. "I never saw him at any of the local pubs. But that does bring something to mind."

"What's that?" I asked, leaning closer.

"There was a story going about that people had seen him in and out of the Lilac in Cork City – ninety miles from here. He might have thought he'd not be recognized there."

"What's the Lilac?" I asked.

"A popular gay pub."

Maureen rolled her eyes. "So....What's the big deal?"

"Because of the Catholic Church's opposition, 'tis a big deal over here, miss."

Dr. Marsten Case came to mind. Could there be a connection? Hadn't Crouch worked in New York where Case lived?

I now had enough confidence in O'Malley's innocence to reveal what we'd learned at the NYAIC. I described our interview with the strange doctors who ran the place, including my take on Dr. Marsten Case's sexual orientation. Then, I disclosed that I was nearly certain I'd seen Resident Magistrate and Rock of Cashel sequestered in one of the import center's barns.

O'Malley jumped up. "Why didn't you tell me, right off?" he shouted, wagging his finger in my face.

IRISH MIST

I brushed his hand aside. "Hold on! I'm not absolutely certain those were the stolen horses, and besides, we'd never met you before. For all we knew, you might be a thief and murderer! And make no mistake – as far as I'm concerned, you're not cleared, yet!"

O'Malley, at loss for words, lowered his head and slumped back down in his chair.

I slowly rose to my feet. "What we've discussed is important, but the problem is that part of this puzzle is here, and the rest in America. Makes our job more difficult....but not impossible."

Maureen shook her head. "And you don't have any real evidence."

"You're right." I paced around, rubbing my hands together. "But, there might be a way to bring the pieces together."

"Simon, don't play Sherlock Holmes with us," Maureen said.

"Okay....Who's McConnell's boss? Where's he stationed?"

"That would be Chief Superintendant Lawrence Walsh," O'Malley said. "He's at Garda Headquarters in Limerick."

I nodded. "I have an idea but, Sean, you're going to have to trust me."

"What is it you want from me?" he asked, shifting in his chair.

Just as I was about to answer, my cell rang, and we

all flinched. I fumbled for my phone. "What is it?" I said, perturbed.

It was Nurse Blake from Galway Hospital. "Yes, I understand....I'll be there first thing in the morning."

Maureen glared. "What was that all about?"

"The nurse at Galway Hospital had a message from P.J. – 'My memory's back. We need to talk.'"

For a moment, we stared at each other.

I folded my arms and studied O'Malley. "Back to my plan....If I can set something up with Chief Superintendant Walsh, I want you to go to Limerick and turn yourself in."

O'Malley leaped to his feet. "What the hell are you talking about?" he shouted. "Are you out of your mind?"

35

Though I hadn't worked out the details, I outlined a plan to O'Malley. Certain electronic equipment would have to be located and installed, then I'd have Frank Reilly contact him. Reluctantly, O'Malley agreed to roll the dice.

When Maureen and I called it a night, I explained that I intended to rise early and return to the hospital and spend the day with P.J. Maureen elected to sleep in, claiming three was a crowd. Maybe later in the day, she would hire a trail horse and enjoy the spectacular ride around nearby *Lough Ree*. Couldn't blame her – this trip had been anything but relaxing. And, why not do some sightseeing and unwind – her horses had been found and hopefully waiting for her at the NYAIC.

In the morning, I gulped down eggs and an English muffin in my room, picked up a roadie coffee in the lobby and found the Renault. As I climbed in, I spotted something on the floor of the passenger side. It was a bullet – probably the one that shattered the rear window. I slipped it in my pocket.

I drove at a snail's pace down the road from St. Clerans, looking for a path into the woods where the shooter might have pulled off and waited for us last night. Just beyond the curve where I'd tossed aside the tree limb, I found muddy car tracks and trampled brush. I parked the Renault along the shoulder. Fifty yards in, I spotted three shell casings on the ground. I picked them up with my handkerchief then took a few digital pictures of the tread imprints, spreading a dollar bill across the marks to establish width.

At eight-thirty, I arrived at the hospital. I waved at the lady on duty and kept moving down the corridor. I was in no mood to be questioned or to wait for permission.

P.J. was watching CNN while a nurse fed her oatmeal.

"How ya doing, beautiful?" I asked.

Though she responded with only a strained smile, today her eyes were open, and some of the swelling in her face had gone down.

The nurse glanced up. "She's grand, sir. Your visit will brighten her day."

I smiled. It warmed my heart to see her improving. "Would it be okay if I fed the patient? Doesn't look too difficult."

"That would be lovely," the nurse said. "Give her water through the straw, if she asks." She pointed to a glass on the table. "Should she cough, give her a pillow to press against her ribs. And if you need assistance, just press the green button."

"I can handle that." I leaned over and kissed P.J.'s forehead.

She switched off the TV. "I'm glad to see you," she said with a twinkle in her eye. The slur in her speech was gone.

I sat down, then dabbed the corner of her mouth with a napkin. She frowned as if hating to be so dependent – particularly on me. I stirred her cereal. "This smells good," I said, presenting a spoonful for her to eat.

"If it's so delicious, why don't you have a bowl with me, Doctor Rush?"

I chuckled. "I'd like to, but I had my breakfast at the hotel."

"The complete Irish one with kippers, I suppose?"

"No, just scrambled eggs and a muffin in my room. Now, tell me what you recall about the vehicle that ran you and Grady Quinn off the road."

She nodded. "When my head cleared, I remembered that same truck at the draft horse show at Kilcolgan. It was an ordinary white lorry, but what struck me as odd, it had a Mercedes Benz hood ornament. I know what a Mercedes hood and grill look like, and that was definitely no Mercedes. And guess who owned it?"

"Who?"

She pushed away a spoonful of oatmeal. "Sergeant Ross McConnell! I was with him at the show!"

"Really!"

"When that truck was ramming us, the driver's face was above my line of sight, but I saw the radiator, and I know that emblem."

"Good work, partner. And I may have found another piece of evidence."

"What?" she asked, sliding up in her bed.

I explained that after our visit to the hospital yesterday, Maureen and I were shot at. And earlier this morning, I located the spot where the shooter had fired from and found three shell casings and photographed the tire tracks.

"We may have a case, if all this evidence points to McConnell," I said.

"Maybe, but none of that proves he stole Resident Magistrate and Rock of Cashel. And what about Fiona McBride? And who killed Doyle Crouch?"

I nodded, collecting my thoughts. "P.J., listen, I want to bounce an idea off you. If we could hold a video conference with McConnell and O'Malley and the NYAIC doctors, it would bring everybody together, and I'm convinced a lot of information would surface."

P.J.'s eyes opened wider. She touched her swathed head and winced. "Could that be done?" she asked.

"I know that the NYAIC has the equipment – I saw it in Helm's office. I'd need to talk to McConnell's superior, Chief Superintendant Walsh, to see what's available at Limerick."

"I like it....with a couple reservations."

"Let's hear 'em."

"What's to keep them from refusing or, if they accept, from skipping out during the interview?" she asked.

"Well, in either case, they'd look even more suspicious."

She nodded.

"What else?" I asked.

"I wouldn't be able to participate!"

I chuckled. "That's no problem. We could hook you in with a conference phone. You wouldn't be able to see, but you could listen and talk. We're going to need your input."

P.J. reached for my hand and smiled. "Simon, remember the first time I said you were brilliant? Back at Trails End Stables. My opinion hasn't changed."

"That's kind of you, my dear. I strive to please."

I scooped up more oatmeal, but she shoved my hand away, spilling some on her bed. "Simon, I have a good feeling about this meeting," she said. "Should we consult an American police officer? We'd need to be able to rely on the legality of any evidence or confession. What about our pal, Detective Stanley Tobin in Ft. Worth – maybe get him involved?"

"Why not?" I said. "We could try. The horses were stolen from Texas buyers so he should have jurisdiction. Let's call him."

It seemed too simple.

P.J. shook her head. "You call, Simon. He'd know by the sound of my voice that something was wrong. Don't mention the....accident. We don't want to complicate this – yet."

"All right. If you feel up to it, I'll do it now?"

"Are you kidding? I'm growing stronger by the minute!"

* * * * * * *

"Stan, this is Simon Rush. I'm with P.J. Porter in Galway, Ireland. Do you have time to talk?"

"I'll make time. How are you guys? This must be important to call me so early and from so far away."

"I'm fine, but P.J.'s got laryngitis. It's too damp over here for her delicate pipes. She's asked me to do the talking."

P.J. punched my arm.

"What can I do for you, Simon?" he asked.

I chronicled the horse thefts and how we ended up in Ireland and why I was proposing a video meeting. There were only a couple of catches – the availability of certain electronics in Limerick and his participation to supervise the NYAIC characters.

He laughed at my pleading. "I think I can help. I was in New York two weeks ago, attending a meeting of the National Association of Bunco Investigators. One of the topics was horse swindles. It's become popular. I have two cases on my desk, and a buddy of mine, Detective Jim Hanrahan with the NYPD, has twice that. These thefts cross jurisdictional lines, so you're talking about a federal issue as well as local."

"Would it be possible for you to come to New York City and take part in a video interrogation?"

"Probably. It's justified, and the FBI has two flights a day going up there. They could even drop me at Rock Tavern. And Jim Hanrahan would jump at the opportunity to join in. What's the name of the guy in charge of NYAIC?"

"Dr. Dante Helm, a tough German," I replied.

"Just tell me when, and we'll be there. Just make sure the Limerick station has the proper stuff."

"Okay. Stan, you're terrific. I'll get back to you in a couple of hours."

"Give my best to P.J." He hung up.

* * * * * * *

An hour and a half later, I was sitting across from Chief Superintendant Walsh at the police station in Limerick. I presented him with the bullet and the three cartridges and the memory card from my digital camera, picturing the vehicle tracks.

More importantly, I pledged to deliver Sean O'Malley to him at 3:45 pm, day after tomorrow, if he'd agree to a video meeting with the NYAIC and have Sergeant McConnell there. He readily accepted the plan but had to contact his TV supplier to install a Webcam and microphone. At the same time, he arranged conference call capability with the hospital. Once these hurdles were cleared, I telephoned Detective Tobin.

"We're good to go here, Stan," I reported.

"Simon, I used to think P.J. Porter was too good for you, but I'm about to change my mind!"

36

Maureen and I had a day to kill before the video conference.

When she'd rented a horse for her ride around *Lough Ree,* she'd met a riding-instructor/horse-agent, Gilbert Gillfoyle, who'd invited her to spend the next day exploring County Galway. They rode over the land where Fiona McBride had drowned. I'd like to have seen that myself. After lunch, they visited three breeding farms – one was Jimmy Craigh's where Resident Magistrate and Rock of Cashel were foaled.

I was pleased she was occupied. It allowed me the freedom to review details with P.J. and make some calls to firm up the Internet meeting. However, I'd wager that before the sun set, Gillfoyle would try to sell Maureen something – hopefully, just a horse.

P.J. was in good spirits. She was pumped up over the meeting – anxious to have her questions answered and to make a contribution. After all, this had been her case.

From her room, I phoned Chief Superintendant Walsh in Limerick. He assured me he'd installed the necessary electronics and that Sergeant McConnell would be there.

Detective Hanrahan had strong-armed Doctors Helm and Case at the NYAIC to participate in the meeting, and Detective Stan Tobin was flying from Ft. Worth to Rock Tavern to make a timely appearance.

Despite the short notice, the video meeting was on.

The morning of the conference, I'd planned to meet Maureen at eight-thirty in the manor lobby. After five minutes of nervous pacing, I called her room. No answer. The desk clerk suggested I check the dining room. There she was – sipping coffee and exchanging giggles with Gilbert Gillfoyle. Flaunting long, slicked back hair, he reminded me of an old-time movie star. And why was he still in riding breeches and boots? Had they gone for a midnight gallop?

From the doorway, I motioned for her to wrap it up. We had to be in Limerick in an hour and a half.

Chief Walsh, resplendent in dress blues and waxed gray mustache, escorted us into his office. He seated us at a round table with a microphone and a telephone and a wireless keyboard placed in the center.

The paneling was stained oak. A fifty inch, plasma TV hung on one wall with its webcam pointing at the table.

Once we were settled, Walsh said, "Excuse me a moment."

He opened the door to an adjoining office, peered

inside and beckoned. "Gentlemen, please join us."

Sean O'Malley and a policeman, presumably Sergeant McConnell, shuffled into our midst. O'Malley and the officer sat down, looking around, sizing up the situation.

Walsh had everyone introduce themselves, then paused and folded his hands on the table. "Well....Mr. Rush persuaded me to conduct this video meeting with New York. We hope to determine whether Sean O'Malley, here, is guilty of misappropriating the show horses he sold to Miss Farrell."

He glanced at Maureen, who solemnly nodded, then he continued. "The two stolen horses were supposed to have been flown to New York City then moved to the New York Animal Import Center at Rock Tavern for medical screening. Mr. Rush and I have arranged for a video connection with the NYAIC. Miss P.J. Porter, who's been recovering in the Galway City Hospital, has been spliced in. Now, I'm going to turn the meeting over to Mr. Rush."

I started to rise, changed my mind and slid back in my chair. "Thank you, Chief," I said. "P.J. can you hear me?"

Her voice came over the mike. "Loud and clear."

"Good. Now, to make the Internet link with New York."

Pulling the keyboard toward me, I punched in the NYAIC's nine digit code. Seconds later, Dr. Helm's office appeared on our monitor. A remarkable picture. Oh, the wonder of modern electronics!

In the middle of a rectangular table sat Doctors Dante Helm and Marsten Case, facing each other, with Detectives Stan Tobin and Jim Hanrahan at the far end.

It was good to see the calm and thoughtful Stan Tobin, a bit more bald and wearing his usual rumpled blue suit. Though Hanrahan had a full thatch, his worn, stretched tie told me he was cut from the same fabric as Stan. Still, if the doctors thought they were dealing with rubes, they were in for a surprise.

I faced the New York group on the monitor. "Gentlemen, can you see and hear me?"

"Picture and sound are perfect," Stan replied, waving at me.

Once names and job descriptions were exchanged, I thanked everyone for agreeing to participate. "We're trying to figure out what happened to Resident Magistrate and Rock of Cashel, the two show horses Miss Farrell purchased from Sean O'Malley.

"Mr. O'Malley voluntarily turned himself in to Chief Superintendant Walsh and has agreed to participate with the understanding he *might* benefit from this meeting."

Dr. Helm interrupted, rapping on the table. "What has this to do with us, Mr. Rush? Need I remind you, we're very busy here!"

I raised my hand. "Patience please, Dr. Helm. This shouldn't take long."

Turning toward McConnell, I said, "Let's get started. Sergeant, it's my understanding you've accused Sean

IRISH MIST

O'Malley of stealing the Farrell horses. Will you explain why?"

McConnell shifted in his seat. "Well....when we were assigned the case, we interrogated O'Malley. Later, we attempted to recall him for a second interview, but he'd vanished."

"Who's *we*?" I interrupted.

"Ah, meself and Deputy Fitzgerald."

"All right, go ahead," I said.

"When we found O'Malley's cap and abandoned truck at the Cilffs of Moher," McConnell said. "We concluded he'd committed suicide because he was guilty and undone by the consequences.

"After a week passed, we recovered a body from the ocean, but it was Doyle Crouch's, not O'Malley's. This added suspicion of murder."

"Sergeant, did you have any other evidence or suspects?" I asked.

"Not at that point," he replied.

O'Malley jumped up, shaking his fist at McConnell. "Why'd you tell everyone, including the newspaper, that you were sure I'd swindled the Farrells when you had no real proof? You were supposed to be my friend!"

P.J. interrupted over the speaker. "Sergeant, I have another question. You were acquainted with Fiona McBride, were you not?"

"Yes, I was."

"Were you in the horse breeding business with her?"

P.J. asked.

McConnell wrung his hands. "From time to time, I was, yes."

"So you knew her well?"

"Ah....I did."

Maureen glanced at me. We were both surprised he'd wasted no time owning up to this, and his body language revealed no sign of guilt. Could we have misjudged this man?

P.J. pushed on. "Sergeant, on a different matter, I was riding behind you during the Blazer Anniversary Hunt when Fiona McBride crashed and drowned."

"Oh...." McConnell's face paled.

"When she was about to jump the ditch, you cracked your whip which spooked her horse, causing it to come up short and fall back in the water on top of her. Minutes later, you galloped up to me and said you hadn't seen her. Why did you lie?"

The Sergeant's body went rigid, and his face turned even whiter. "P.J., that wasn't me! You're mistaken!"

"You're still lying, McConnell! I was there and saw you!" P.J. yelled.

Chief Walsh motioned for everyone to remain calm. "Sergeant, here and now we're getting to the bottom of this. You're not obligated, but if you're involved or know anything, it will go easier on you if you cooperate."

McConnell looked around, wringing his hands.

I glanced up at the TV monitor. The doctors were

wide-eyed while Tobin and Hanrahan were stone-faced – old timers, accustomed to such confrontations.

"All right!" McConnell declared, striking the table with the palm of his hand. "I saw that the far bank was water soaked and crumbling. I yelled at her to turn and flicked my whip, urging her horse to break off. But Fiona was committed to the jump."

The Sergeant leered at me and Maureen. "Regardless of wrecks and unintended dismounts, hunt tradition demands that we keep up with the Field. If there's a fall or injury, hunt staff should take charge. I had to keep moving!"

Walsh nodded. "'Tis true."

P.J. shot back, "Then why did you say you hadn't seen her?"

The Sergeant's chin dropped. Until this moment, he'd appeared self-assured, but now, his body sagged with anxiety and remorse.

"P.J., I was embarrassed," he admitted, almost to himself. "If you saw the accident, I knew you wouldn't understand why I rode off. I didn't want to appear unfeeling."

Long seconds passed. Then P.J. said calmly, "Let's put that aside for a minute....Sergeant, weren't you driving the truck with the Mercedes hood ornament that ran Grady Quinn and me off the road?"

Maureen gasped.

McConnell closed his eyes and murmured. "I don't

know what you're talking about."

He would be foolish to admit to ramming us. At a minimum, he'd be facing manslaughter. But I didn't want this interrogation to be delayed while he lawyered-up. Keep it moving, I thought.

"McConnell, there's something else you should know," I interjected. "Chief Walsh has ballistic proof that it was your service rifle that was used to shoot at me and Miss Farrell at St. Clerans. There's also tire track evidence!" I leaned forward and glared at him. "Sergeant, what's going on?"

The Chief shook his index finger in McConnell's face and shouted, "Come now, man! Out with it or we're through, and I'll lock you up!"

The Sergeant glanced toward heaven, as if praying *that this cup might pass*. "All right! But, I swear on my mum's grave, I did not intend to hurt anyone. I just wanted you and P. J. to get out of Ireland!"

"That's insane! What possessed you?" the Chief yelled, jumping to his feet.

It took all my will power not to strangle McConnell.

He shook his head and mumbled, "I was.... threatened."

"What the hell do you mean you were *threatened*?" I shouted, shaking my fist.

"Who threatened you?" Walsh demanded.

The Sergeant placed one hand on the table, and the other on top of it. He appeared to be wrestling with how much more to say. But that wasn't my concern. He was a police officer and knew his rights. Finally, he said, "Doyle Crouch had warned me that our lives were in danger if we so much as hinted to anyone about the horse scam. After Crouch was murdered, I got a phone call. A guy with an accent warned me that I'd be next if I didn't force P.J. to go home."

Walsh leaned forward and glared. "What kind of accent?"

"Foreign....I'm not sure."

Maureen jumped in. "What makes you think Crouch was murdered?"

"The autopsy indicated he'd been garroted, Russian Mafia style, then tossed off the Cliffs."

Russian Mafia! Where was this going? "Are you saying it was some sort of hit?" I asked.

"I think so," McConnell replied.

"What was Crouch's roll in all this?"

"He directed everything but took orders from someone higher up – maybe a foreigner."

"What do you mean 'directed everything?'" I asked.

The Sergeant hesitated.

Chief Walsh stabbed his finger at him. "Speak up man. You're in trouble here, but the more you cooperate, the more support you'll get from me!"

McConnell winced at our relentless prodding. "Over the past three years, Crouch fleeced a number of foreign buyers with bogus horses from Limerick, Clare and Galway

Counties. Fiona McBride supplied the lookalikes, and he acquired phony passports and handled the shipping. This was all carried out while he was Head Inspector at Shannon Airport."

"What was your role?" I demanded.

"Crouch hired me for protection, but none was needed – 'til now."

O'Malley shook his head in disgust. "You son of a bitch!" he murmured.

Ignoring this well deserved footnote, I asked, "Who switched the microchips?"

"That was performed somewhere else – I'm not sure – maybe at the destinations."

I rose and walked around the table, whispered in the Chief's ear, "Can we talk in the next room?"

I looked up at the monitor. "Gentlemen, would you give us a minute?"

The detectives nodded. The doctors scowled.

37

Once the Chief shut the door, I flipped open my cell phone and called P.J. "Chief Superintendant Walsh and I ducked out of the meeting. We're in another office. I wanted to get your take on McConnell."

"He's intimidated and trying to save his skin," she said. "But he's not the kingpin."

I nodded. "Do you think he's been telling the truth?"

"Yes, but I never heard that Doyle Crouch was the object of a mob hit. Ask the Chief what he knows about that."

I turned to Walsh. "Chief, were you aware that Crouch was garroted by a pro? And what would make Sergeant McConnell suggest it was a Russian Mafia style hit?"

"That was news to me," he said, shaking his head. "I've not seen the autopsy report, yet – takes time to go through channels. But a mob strangulation is distinctive – a crushed trachea is one hundred percent effective."

P.J. changed the subject. "McConnell mentioned the microchip switch was not done in Ireland – probably in the U.S. That's what you figured with your Preparation H theory. Simon, I think it's time to interrogate the doctors."

"You're right. It's time."

"While you're at it," P.J. said, "ask them if Resident Magistrate and Rock of Cashel are currently being held at the NYAIC. That should shake things up, big time."

"Okay. Good idea."

"But avoid admitting how you obtained the information," she added. "Breaking and entering would make it inadmissible."

I'd have to think of something in a hurry.

"I'll try," I said, then glanced at Walsh. "Ready, Chief?"

He tweaked his mustache. "You're running this thing. Let's go."

I signed off with P.J. and followed Chief Walsh back into the conference room. As we seated ourselves, the Chief looked at the monitor and announced, "Sorry. We had a small matter to clear up. Resume, Mr. Rush, please."

I caught a glimpse of the screen. The doctors and even the detectives appeared annoyed and anxious for me to wrap it up. But this was my show, and I wasn't about to be pushed.

"About switching the microchips," I said. "I believe Resident Magistrate's and Rock of Cashel's chips were extracted, then injected into the necks of Local Judge and Hard Cash, without leaving a trace. Dr. Helm, can you explain how that could be done?"

Helm's chin jutted, and his eyes flashed. "I don't know what you're talking about! When you were here, I told you that only two Farrell horses, whose chips were authenticated, passed through the NYAIC and were routinely picked up by their transport agent. That was the end of it!"

"Dr. Helm, what if I told you I had reliable information that, at this very moment, Rock of Cashel and Resident Magistrate are being held captive in one of your quarantine barns?"

The doctor flushed and jumped to his feet. "Are you mad, Rush? That can't be!" He glared at his associate. "Marsten, what's he talking about? Do you know anything?"

Helm paused, then began shaking his finger at his colleague, slow at first, then furiously. "Wait a minute! A while back, you asked if I thought a microchip could be removed with a biopsy needle." Helm's eyes narrowed. "What the hell's going on here, Case?"

Dr. Case's face paled, and, even on the monitor, I could see his body begin to quiver. I thought he was going to faint.

Helm moved close and grabbed him by the collar. "Tell us! Are the Farrell horses in one of our barns?"

Detective Tobin jumped up and clutched Helm's

shoulders, forcing him back in his chair.

"They were," Case whimpered. "But they're gone now."

"Who took them?" Tobin roared.

Case buried his head in his hands and whispered, "I was ordered to release the horses to a transport agent."

Dr. Helm punched his shoulder. "Louder, man! Who gave that order?"

Case's chin dropped against his chest, and he began to sob. "Crouch and I were threatened, too. Then Doyle wanted out – a fatal mistake."

Stan leaned over and lifted his chin. "Dr. Case, help yourself! Stay with us! Who gave the order to discharge the horses? Who picked them up?"

Case slowly raised his head, took a deep breath and turned toward the monitor. "Tex Farrell ran this scheme! His agent took delivery of the horses yesterday afternoon."

Deathly silence fell over both rooms.

I looked at Maureen. Her eyes glazed over. "Oh lord – no! Daddy, why?" she gasped. Then, dropping her head into her hands, she began to weep, tears gushing down her cheeks and her body shaking with every breath. "Oh, Daddy....Oh, Daddy....Oh, Daddy!" she repeated, over and over.

If she wasn't genuinely grieved, she was one hell of an actress.

No wonder Tex didn't want us flying to Ireland.

P.J.'s incredulous voice boomed over the microphone,

"Oh – my – God!"

Chief Walsh gave me a bearhug and whispered in my ear, "Grand performance, my boy."

* * * * * * *

Maureen, still shaken, called a cab and headed for the airport. She'd declined to discuss anything, and Chief Superintendant Walsh had no grounds to detain her.

Her parting words caught me by surprise. "You and P.J. earned the hundred thousand – I'll see that you get it."

Whether she was involved in the swindle, I'd leave to Detectives Tobin and Hanrahan. I hoped she wasn't.

Sergeant Ross McConnell was jailed for his participation. The nature of the charges, including the extent of his culpability for the deaths of Grady Quinn and Fiona McBride, would be up to the Magistrate. Whether McConnell was the father of Fiona's fetus would probably never be known.

The Chief patted O'Malley on the shoulder. "You're free to go, Sean," he said. But judging from O'Malley's twisted grin, I'm sure he expected more – like a thorough apology.

I spent the better part of an hour with Chief Superintendant Walsh, reviewing the case. He asked that P.J. and I make ourselves available, at Ireland's expense, for any depositions, arraignments or trials, and, of course, we agreed. He was more than appreciative of our service to his department and, in return, promised to help expedite the payment of the seventy thousand euros we'd earned from Lloyds of London.

Next to Tex Farrell, McConnell was the biggest surprise to me. I figured it boiled down to selfishness and greed. Irish police sergeants probably didn't make much, so a chance to supplement his income would be a powerful temptation. But, as long as McConnell lived, in or out of jail, he'd regret his participation in this fraud that seemed doomed to failure from the beginning.

As for Farrell, he had to go along with Maureen's idea of upping the Lloyds of London reward money in order to maintain his appearance of innocence. But ironically, it was P.J.'s pursuit of the money that did him in.

He was one of the richest men in Texas. If I had to speculate, it was the challenge or thrill of outsmarting the mighty insurance companies for which he must have held a monstrous grudge. To him, it was a game – like an evil chess match that spun out of control once Doyle Crouch was killed. Disposing of Crouch was the ultimate checkmate intended not only to silence Crouch but also to keep Sergeant McConnell and Dr. Case in line.

How Tex induced Crouch and Case to do his dirty work was a mystery. Was there a homosexual relationship or incident that he discovered and exploited? Or could Farrell himself have been involved in an unnatural triad?

And proving Farrell was responsible for hiring the hit man to eliminate Crouch would be difficult.

But these mind-bogglers would be up to Detectives Tobin and Hanrahan to unravel, back in the U.S.

I arrived at the hospital around dinner time. A flower shop across the street was open, so I picked up a bouquet of mixed daisies.

P.J. had guests – Sean O'Malley and a pleasant surprise, her father, Dr. Guy Porter. Before I could shake hands, P.J. motioned to me with one open arm. "Thanks for the posies. Simon, you were wonderful!"

"So were you, beautiful!"

She pulled me down and gave me a messy but wonderful kiss that tasted of mashed potatoes. No matter – it told me everything I needed to know. Our relationship had weathered the Maureen storm. And if we wanted a future together, the possibility was there.

O'Malley was generous with his thanks to P.J. and me for clearing him and restoring his reputation. When he rose to leave, he said, "I know you two have lots of catching up to do." He opened the door, then turned back. "I almost forgot….Kit and Barbara Devereux send their congratulations. Also, they want both of you to prepare expense reports, covering everything, including P.J.'s medical bills. They'll take care of all of it."

"How generous! We'll do that," I said, surprised to be included. After all, P.J. had been hired by them – I was a mere volunteer.

Once O'Malley'd left, Dr. Porter rose and ambled toward the door. "I'm going down the hall to make a few phone calls. And you two need a few minutes together."

"Hurry back," P.J. said with a wave. I was pleased she'd made no effort to stop him.

I noticed there were still a few blotches of black and blue on her brow and jaw. "To look at me," she said, squeezing my hand, "you'd never guess this has been the best day of my life! I'm feeling better, the case is solved and my wonderful dad came three thousand miles to comfort me....and you're here, too, Simon."

Then she added, "And my father brought the most exciting news!"

She was radiant.

"What news?"

"Transport is out of the clinic and spending two hours a day in the pasture."

"Oh, P.J., that's great! When you get home, the two of you can heal together. And hey! I've got an idea! I'll come by each morning and feed both of you your breakfast oats."

She laughed and beckoned to me again. "Come over here you! Let's try that kiss again!"

THE END

ACKNOWLEDGEMENTS

This is my fifth book. To my surprise, each one has needed as much research, outside help and editing as the one before. Conclusion: the author's name is on the cover, but it takes a village to produce the end result.

The prominent citizens of my hamlet are:

Editing and storyline – Carolyn Wall, my extraordinary mentor.

Editing and encouragement – Hiram Myers, Karen Browne, Phyllis Stough and Marilyn Meade.

Equine medicine – Dr. William C. Edwards, D.V.M.

Police protocol – Chief Richard Mask of the Nichols Hills Police Department, and Lieutenant Bruce Davis and Master Sergeant Robin Snavely of the Oklahoma City Police Department.

Special kudos – Eoin Ryan from Dundalk, County Louth, Ireland for all facts and background Irish, and to William Henry, who in 1999 wrote numerous booklets which recounted the colorful history of St. Clerans and its owners. These accounts were placed in the manor suites and changed weekly for the enlightenment and entertainment of the guests.